THE SHAPE OF CLOUDS

ALMA BOOKS LTD
London House
243–253 Lower Mortlake Road
Richmond
Surrey TW9 2LL
United Kingdom
www.almabooks.com

First published by Hodder and Stoughton in 1996
This edition published by Alma Books Limited in 2012
Copyright © Peter Benson, 1996

Peter Benson asserts his moral right to be identified as the author of
this work in accordance with the Copyright, Designs and Patents Act
1988

Cover image © Ged Cowburn

Printed and bound by CPI Group (UK) Ltd, Croydon, CR0 4YY

Typeset by Tetragon

ISBN: 978-1-84688-197-8

THE SHAPE OF CLOUDS

PETER BENSON

ALMA BOOKS

1

On thin and watery days the road to Port Juliet dissolves into the land. It fades and only the sky remains, and the sea as it breaks over the offshore stacks. The air lightens, clouds rise, the road forgets. Sheep forget to graze, and a single cow stares at the weather, the rocks and the grass.

But if the weather changes, if clouds lower from the west and rain curtains across the fields, then the road stands out like a ribbon blown across a woman's face, or a curl of grey hair, and its bends wave to the ruins and my house. It fails and dies at the shore. It does itself no favours.

Bordered by broken stone walls, old trees bent eastward by the wind, rutted and potholed in patches that have spread like disease, the road has no signpost standing. Crows gather in the trees and watch the rocky fields that patch the land, and the ruts run with water. Thin land, salty air, winds like shears. Blanket rain and clouds that hang like granite in a cut sky. The road to Port Juliet is an old road but forgotten; it's the line from a film I fell in love with but haven't seen for thirty-five years.

Once Port Juliet supported a farmer, a pair of weavers, mussel-growers and an artist who came to paint the clouds as they rolled in from the ocean. Postmaster Mr Boundy of Zennack told me everything. He waited until the shop was empty, then took off his glasses and joined me in his intrusive way on the customer side of the counter. It was very important that I knew, that I was told and made to understand. He wagged his finger and licked his lips in anticipation of my response. These are foreign parts and strangers must be educated and warned. Nothing escapes. Everything is noticed, and the portents are read. I am alone and old. I am a gift for Mr Boundy and the locals, with no Post Office savings book or any letters arriving at all. I can be anyone they want, some perfect nightmare washed up on their shore, living in a ruin at the edge of nowhere with a dog that is half horse, whose bark can knock rocks off the cliffs.

The artist painted Port Juliet for a month then left, beaten back to London by a wind that tore the roof from his house, and rain that filled his bed. He managed to complete half a dozen pictures. One of these used to hang in the National Gallery. *Port Juliet after the Tempest* is an atmospheric watercolour, painted in the hours after the village had been shaken by the wildest gales for years. Mr Boundy's seen it. A curl of cloud is all that can be discerned of the storm; this hangs like a scar in the lightening sky. The sea is calming and birds can be made out over the offshore stacks. Used to hang... The painting was removed to the gallery's basement in 1983, and has not been shown since. Mr Boundy did not stop talking — he told me that he had wanted to buy the picture to hang over the counter of the Zennack post office by the premium bonds advertisement, but no, don't be ridiculous. As the painting, as the artist, so the place. Shot and gutted and hung out to dry at the edge of England, the port that never was a port. Twitching, one eye half open, a gobby mouth and bad teeth.

These ruins — a few houses and barns — stand at the neck of a point of land that drops into the ocean five miles west of Zennack. West as feet can follow, the sea a pool of all the tears that were shed over the place. My house stands beyond the ruins, and faces the mile of sand that curves to the cliff path and the point.

The last farmer who lived in Port Juliet went insane, and his sheep went insane with him. With their fleeces like rubbish and their flesh like wood, and their heads filled with vague dreams of other fields; when the last farmer took them to market he was laughed away. He was told to give up but he could not, and wept as he collected the pittance he was owed. See the grown man cry... Mr Boundy had been a boy but remembered the incident well. The farmer recognised himself in his animal's looks, and he saw all his despair swarming behind their eyes. He walked away from Zennack and never returned to Port Juliet. He caught a bus to Penzance and no one heard about him again. 'I'll never forget his tears,' Mr Boundy told me, 'or his look. Not if I live to be a hundred.'

Two of the farmhouse walls remain, and a fireplace. I can see them from my kitchen window. The outline of the stables can be seen in the dirt, and the steel frame of the screwed barn, but the sheets of corrugated iron that made its walls have been scattered by the wind, left to flip into the sea or the marshy ground behind the house. Here too are the old bones of sheep who strayed and sank on a summer night under a full moon, says Mr Boundy.

So tears and insanity drove the farmer away, and his wife and all their children moved east to her family's home. The weavers followed, looking for warmer houses and finer fleeces, and then there were only the mussel-growers, and they abandoned the place after storms ripped their poles from the seabed and tossed their pieces into the race beyond the point, apparently.

Once, the weavers worked at their windows with views of the beach and the ocean, but now the windows are gone, jemmied out and taken to allotments in Zennack where they were given a coat of non-toxic paint and turned into cold-frames for lettuce and other vegetable seedlings. 'Come on, I'll show you.' And the doors are gone, and the floorboards, and the galvanised tubs that used to sit out the back to collect rainwater. And the chicken arks, and the sheds where fleeces were stored. Only the walls of the houses remain, and some pieces of broken glass. Not even ghosts wander through the places that were once crowded with people, and hummed with the sound of shuttling looms. Ghosts need reasons, and there are none at Port Juliet, only the flakes of old dreams, and old memories.

At night, if the moon has waned and the sea is still, there is no road to Port Juliet, and the ruins cannot be seen. The only light comes from my house, a glow from the kitchen window. It tries to hide behind a sheet of plastic I have tacked over the frame, but cannot. The room is a mess. I wish it wasn't, the chaos goes against my nature, but it's only temporary. Sacks of cement are stacked against one wall, and a pile of rubble, wood shavings and dust is piled in the corner behind the stove. Lengths of wood are propped up behind the larder door. Soon I am going to fix glass in the frame, plaster the walls and lay tiles on the floor, but for now, for now there is little sound, no movement, no one can be heard talking. No one moves across the beach, the ocean fails, the sky is deeper than silence, and deeper than love.

A month ago there were the most terrific calm days. The sea settled like a shroud, and early spring mists covered the fields. The clouds grew slow and light, and drifted like gentle swells on an ocean. I was lazy for a week, and spent my time in lonely contemplation. I didn't work; I ignored the timetable I had drawn up for the vegetable garden. I sat on the stones outside the front door and talked to the dog about places I have been and reasons I have given for walking away from friends I have made. Now the weather has changed. The days are lengthening, the sun is warmer, and I spent all morning digging and hoeing, raking and seeding. On any day I can be watched, and I am. Men and their children come from Zennack and stand on the cliffs to see what I am doing. They never approach, they never wave, the children have been warned, and keep their distance. Some dare their friends, but I am greater than their bravado. They know I can stare a cat to death and that I eat raw meat. My stare can fade colour, and my nose drips acid. I can speak a foreign language backwards, and sweep dirt without a broom. I am the strolling revenant who will never tell the truth, the man who sucks the blood from cows' backs and leaves them to die on moonless nights.

Who am I? Where have I come from? I have told Mr Boundy the truth, and he has told me what people say, and he'll nod and stare and believe that I am lying, whatever I say. Yes, it is true, and everyone knows it: I have killed a man, maybe two. Or I am the son of the weeping farmer, returned to finish what my father began. Or I am deaf. Or a famous man, a composer or writer. I am not a man at all, but a large woman with coarse hair. I am Spanish. I am a disgraced bishop with a box of photographs. I was a spy, and lost my mind in a Bulgarian prison. I was betrayed by people I thought I could trust, I ran for years and now I am hiding. Or I am none of these things, but something far worse. I am a curse, the man Port Juliet has waited for. My breath can blow holes in rain, and suck the marshes dry. I am planting spores in every county of England, and will release them on New Year's Day. I am the shadow of an invisible spectre that always walks two steps ahead of me. People have noticed how cold the air is around me, and how normal dogs shy away from me. I am every dread, every hate, every whisper in the night; the words you will carry to your grave. I steal body parts from living animals, and am using them to build a beast. I am someone who can drink swamps dry. I bleed without pain. I have two tongues; one is yellow and I keep it rolled up in the back of my mouth.

But... but I am none of these things. What I am is a slow worker. Thorough. When I am not rebuilding my house I am growing vegetables, and keeping to myself. My reticence is my threat and my silence breeds mistrust. I don't care that I am watched. People can stare but they cannot touch me. I am beyond them, beyond petty rages, petty ambition, beyond mediocrity. They want to know what I do: all they have to do is look. All they have to do is release themselves. I have never grown vegetables before, but my carrots are showing, and a row of radishes. I am going to repair a cow shed and later in the year I will fill the worst of the potholes in the road with rocks and shingle from the beach. I am sixty-eight. I have waited all my life for a Port Juliet, a house and my place at the edge of the country, and I have waited for love. I have waited for love like a doubting priest waits for God, always walking with my head bowed, never seeing the obvious. I am old enough to know better, old enough not to care. How many times did I run from the obvious? I don't know. How many women have seen me coming? I can't remember. What's the point in remembering? No point at all but it passes the time. Regret? Forget it. I regret nothing, not now. You have changed me.

2

Why does trouble follow a man who lives to avoid it? Because trouble is its own reason, and gives itself a present every day. Like a malignant child with an adult mind, trouble has the power to charm before it strikes. It has a way of smiling that tells you: 'I'm okay, you're okay, we're okay, aren't we?'

I remember: I had been living in Port Juliet for two months. It was autumn. I visited Zennack to shop. I was in the post office buying tinned goods, staring hard at Mrs Boundy. Suddenly she paled, gripped the counter, mumbled something and went to the back room. I heard her ask Mr Boundy to do the serving while she had a lie-down. He laughed and said my name. 'Michael?'

'I can't have him looking at me like that. It's those eyes.'

Mr Boundy laughed again, and came to serve me.

I said, 'Have you got rice pudding?'

'Yes.'

'I'll have two tins.'

Mr Boundy fetched them.

'What about dried apricots?'

'No. We don't keep them. There's not much call for them. I could ask when I see the rep, but then we'd have to buy a whole box, and if there's no demand I'm stuck with them.'

'Don't bother.'

Mr Boundy's eyes narrowed. I could see questions queueing behind his pupils, knocking to be let out. Some were big and some were small. I could hear the stronger ones chattering, willing themselves the words they needed. 'Though maybe, I don't know. Dried apricots. I suppose you could make jam with them...'

'Forget it,' I said.

The questions backed off.

I had a tractor parked outside, with a link-box attached. Mud on the wheels, mud on the pedals, a square of foam on the seat. Gloria stood guard beside it, grinning at passers-by.

I bought Gloria from a gypsy who lived on the top road. Some old man with a cart, a pony and a woman who hid under blankets and branches. He carved figures from driftwood, and sold them on street corners. No, I cannot remember his name. He had a past but I didn't want to know about it. All he said was, 'Promise to look after her.' I promised. 'She's a better dog than any promise.' I agreed with that. She hesitated when I called her but the gypsy said, 'Get on with you,' and she followed me.

'Dog food,' I said.

'Yes...' Mr Boundy left the counter, fetched a ladder, set it against the shelves and climbed. He was up among the tins and said, 'How many?'

'A dozen.'

He brought them down, and a sack of bone-shaped biscuits.

'I don't want biscuits. She doesn't eat them. They hurt her teeth.'

'There must be something wrong with her.'

'She's fine,' I said.

'Okay.' Mr Boundy scratched his face and put them back. 'Anything else?'

'No.'

He began to total the amount. I turned and looked out of the window.

The sun shone on the tractor and the post office of Zennack, and Gloria lay down in the road. A couple of men left the pub, shook hands and walked away from each other. The local taxi drove by, and the driver waved. Mrs Bell came from the only guest house in town, and watered her window boxes. She looked towards the post office. I knew she knew I was there, but I didn't want to see her. Her eyes betray her desire and I think that desire is a handyman, a pair of boots on the kitchen mat, someone to change plugs, Mr Boundy said. 'Ten fifty-five.' I fished for the money and put it on the counter.

A bus stopped outside the church, and a gang of schoolchildren got off. One of them threw a football into the air and chased it down the pavement, into the road and around the cars parked in the square. Three girls broke away and crossed to the post office. As they opened the door I came out with my shopping, Gloria stood up and they were caught between us. The first looked up at me, her face paled and she screamed. I had said nothing. The other two stared at my teeth and my eyes, and my hair, and they froze. They'd heard about me, and it was true. My dog could eat your mother. I was the man in the cupboard at night at the top of the stairs, around the corner before the landing, and my hands were huge and cut from the tools I use. One stared at my mouth while the other looked down and saw a knife hanging from my belt. Gloria took one step forward. The girls let out gasps of air. I could smell them, like grass clippings. Gloria took another step. The girls reached for each other, then turned and ran to their friend who was waiting around the corner with some boys she'd called.

I heard them cry, 'He's horrible!'

'It's true! There was blood on his knife!'

'Real blood. It was dripping...'

'Down his leg...'

'I know!'

'Into his boots!'

'And I could see his other tongue! It was yellow!'

'And his dog! His dog's mad!'

I loaded my shopping into the link-box and whistled to Gloria. I saw Mrs Bell start to walk towards me. I raised my hand and waved to her, but before she was close enough to call without drawing attention to herself, I had turned the tractor around and headed out of the square, left at the chapel and on to the top road.

As I drove and watched the shadows of clouds drip across the fields and into the sea, I thought that the purpose of dreams is to disappoint. Once I had dreamt of having children, but now all I did was scare them. Once I dreamt of a constant life, a house in a row of houses, a job on land, flowers in a garden. Once I thought I was going to get married, and I was ready to. Her name was Isabel and she was a tall woman, as tall as me. She wore cotton dresses and worked for her father, cleaning the house I stayed in: I was going to marry her in Barcelona and buy a café behind the waterfront, but that had been a dream, a sailor's mistake, and the years ambushed me. They stalked me and caught me when I was not expecting it; was the ambush in the South China Sea or Aden or in Buenos Aires? I don't remember, and I don't care any more. Regret wastes time, it drains the head. Only work makes sense.

In the gap between then and whatever happens next, I will not stop rebuilding my house. I have a cement mixer in a shed. The roof's finished and the chimney works. I have laid new pipes from the spring; the water comes slowly from the taps, but is fresh and pure. It is safe to cook on the stove, and the wall behind the fireplace is plastered.

There is a bed upstairs, and a sink in a cupboard on the landing. Gloria has a basket, and there is a painting of a sailing ship on the hall wall. It hangs beside the door, next to a row of hooks. My cap and coat hang here, and a shopping bag.

3

I do not remember my father. My mother never said his name to me. I know he was a curse, a low note in a bad song no one sings any more. I was told by a drunk uncle that his name was Ralph. There could be some saint, a perfect man called Ralph, but I couldn't stay in the same room as him. He could be smiling and carrying flowers but I'd feel some rage building in me, the rage I know very well indeed. It has saved my life, and threatened it. I don't blame my father for anything; weak people mean nothing to me. He left before my birth, before the midwife shook her head over me and told my mother that I would be the luckiest child in town. Luckier than Robert and Diane Grey, next door's children, and they were very lucky children indeed.

Robert and Diane had been riding down the West Ferry Road in their father's delivery van. He had swerved suddenly to avoid a road-sweeper, the back doors had opened and the children had been thrown out, into the path of a bus. They went under the bus.

The driver braked and fainted. Passengers flew from their seats; the conductor's pouch sprayed loose change. People on the top deck screamed, and a woman in a hat began to gibber. One pedestrian went to a telephone, and another yelled for a doctor. Mr Grey leapt from his van and ran to the bus.

He yelled madly, and as he did, the children crawled out and stood up. They were untouched. Their elbows weren't even grazed. A devout husband and wife came from a grocer's shop and went down on their knees. Lucky Robert and Diane were talked about for years, and pointed out to strangers. Once, a sick man was brought to them to be touched, to be healed, but Mrs Grey drew the line at that. 'Who do you think we are?'

I will be the luckiest child in town because I was born in my caul. I can spit on water, walk on it, give it flowers. I'll never sail a sinking ship, and every port I visit will know my name. I am special, I am touched, I will never be drowned. It's that simple.

My mother knew about luck. She spat over her left shoulder, clicked the wind away with her fingers, took my caul, wrapped it in a lint-free cloth and carried it home. She wiped it and dried it slowly and carefully, and when it had shrunk to the size of a slice of bread, sewed it into the lining of a man's leather cap. She rocked my cradle and sang a song for the dead in my ear. A song for the living or one for the dead, it never mattered to me.

Nothing touched me, hurt me or changed my mind. I grew up in London, on the Isle of Dogs. I had a view of the river from my room, and could sit day or night and watch ships arrive, dock, unload, reload and leave. I watched the sailors come and I watched them go, and I copied their walk. The tides were my clock, and navigation lights blinked for me. I knew every tug by name, and every line flag that ever sailed up the Thames to the West India Dock, Greenland, South Dock or Shadwell.

I was a strong boy and if other boys wanted to talk about why my father (Ralph) was not living on Strafford Street I would kick them in the knee and warn them that when he returned from a voyage to India and Australia, then he would nail their feet to the trapdoors on the pavement outside the Dock and Chain. As soon as I could think, I knew what I would do. Mother never told me that my father was a seaman but I knew that, somewhere, somehow, and I would be a seaman too.

11

One day, Mother was down the road talking to Mrs Rodden of the baker's shop. I was alone in the house. I was six. It was just before the war.

I went upstairs to her dressing table, and sat on the stool. I looked at her powder compact, and ran her brush through my hair. She had a bottle of perfume, but I didn't touch this. I looked at myself in the mirror, licked some crumbs from the corner of my mouth, and then I went through the drawers.

The top drawer was full of underwear. I caught my sleeve on a hook on the back of something, and couldn't get untangled. I pulled and all this stuff fell on to the floor, corsets and bras and belts all snarled up on my sweater. I had to get down from the stool to sort this mess out. I was standing in the middle of the room picking these frightening clothes off my clothes. They had so many clips and buckles and the more I tried the worse it got. I sat on the floor and concentrated on one corset at a time, then another, then a belt, and I took them carefully and dropped them in the drawer before they did any more damage.

I opened the second drawer. There was a cardigan in it, some pullovers and a nightdress. Some mothballs rattled in the corner. I lifted the nightdress out, and held it to my face. It had lace around the collar. I smelt it. It was cotton, and very light. I put it back and rummaged under the other things, but I couldn't find what I was looking for.

The bottom drawer was difficult to open. It contained three shoe boxes.

There was a dried bouquet in the first box, with a message attached. I couldn't read the words. I touched one of the flowers and its petals dusted under my fingers. A money spider froze on one of the stems. Carnations and roses, all faded and over.

The second box was heavy, and full of jewels. I know these were paste and gilt, but when I was in my mother's room on that day I thought I had discovered the wealth of London. My eyes watered, the jewels sparkled. I could hear them singing, calling out in song, giving me instruction. I shut the box quickly, and pushed it to the back of the drawer.

The third box contained a paper bag. I opened it and the man's leather cap was inside. My heart jumped, and then beat faster. I thought I heard someone coming in the back door; I stood still and listened, but I had been mistaken. The wind, the cat, a stray dog...I was shaking but took the cap out of the bag and sat back on the stool, and turned it over in my hands.

It was black with a handsome peak, and a thin strip of leather running around the rim at the back to a button at the front. It was lined with calfskin and cotton, and I could feel something through this, hard and ridged like a hand. I held it to my nose. It smelled of fog and dust, and something acid.

I smiled at myself in Mother's dressing-table mirror, and then I crowned myself with the cap. It covered my eyes and the back of it sat on my collar. I tipped it back and to one side, and ran my fingers along its peak. I whistled at my reflection, and winked at my smile.

I knew again. I knew who I was and how I was going to sea, and how one day I would end up old and alone in a place like Port Juliet. Born old. Never be fooled.

I knew this knowledge would detach me. I would never be like other people, and they would confuse my certainty with pride. Or arrogance. Or a bad temper. I've got a temper but only fools see it. Maybe I am too quick to judge, maybe I see fools everywhere, but maybe I am right to. At sea in storms with loads of shifting timber, or steel, or with broken pumps and filling bilges, then you have to have a temper, you have to know who the fools are. You do not sail every ocean for fifty years with only a caul in your cap. Luck is conscious. It needs friends, it wants to know you care.

4

I have eaten lizard in Singapore, and been knifed in Odessa. I felt the blade kiss my bones, and pain screamed through two thousand miles to be with me. I had wished that pain on myself though I never deserved it. At that time my mind was bent rigid by guilt. I had been a neglectful son, and had punished myself by inviting trouble. I wanted to be hurt and humiliated in public, I wanted people to see that I was a bad man, and I wanted the severest sentence. I didn't think but I lived, and this is the scar.

In Marseille I took another man's wife to bed. In Lisbon I met a woman who did things to me I could not write about, things with food and electrical equipment, and other instruments from a bosun's stories. Limassol is a port for stories, and Haifa. I've been with women in Haifa who treated me like I was their dream come true, who kissed with a mouthful of wine and never spilt a drop. Who charmed beasts and dusted themselves with sugar and wrapped themselves in nothing but shade.

Sea voyages make men dream beyond reason. The name of the next port will sound like a bell, and the ones left behind whisper the sorrow of partings in sleeping ears. Felixstowe, Hamburg, Dubai, Fujayrah, Karachi, Bombay, Colombo. Barcelona and the beach cafés of Sant Feliu de Guixols. Bells, whispers and women.

No one has told me why Port Juliet is called a port. There are no ruined quays or the scattered remains of warehouses. I have not found the skeleton of a hulk buried in the sand, or rusted chains below the tideline. There are no broken derricks, split pallets or piles of discarded sacks. I would speak to Mr Boundy about this place's name but I'd rather not ask questions. If he wants to tell me he will. And he will. He cannot keep quiet. Maybe, in return, I will tell him about Elizabeth Green, but then he will have to ask the right questions, and I will need to be drinking as I talk. Yes, the Elizabeth Green, the blonde from *Missing You* who made one great film and that was it. The fierce one who had never been a legend, who was not Joan Crawford or Lauren Bacall, who had always missed the best scripts. Who had glimpsed that immortality, the glimpse that maims, the one that kills but spills no blood. Who had disappeared for years, gone so long people thought she was dead, but she wasn't, she was back, she had been rediscovered. Old and gorgeous. Her new film was called *Raintown*. What a lovely title. Elizabeth Green with a black dress and a blue silk scarf tied loosely around her neck. The one I knew and loved years before she knew me. The sailor's wife is the sailor's wrist, but the wrist needs a picture. The picture: a diamond brooch twinkling on her chest, and diamond teardrops hanging from her ears. A bloom of expensive perfume, a light dusting of powder, lipstick. A velvet purse. Coming down the road, picking a stray piece of cotton off her sleeve, coming to make my life complete. Things like this do not happen. They are dreams. My dream, your dream, their dream, the dream fulfilled. Out of the nowhere. Smaller in real life, and louder. Asking for a phone. A vision of love in the place I want, and that place is my home.

Our street was bombed in the war. Mother had refused to leave; we emerged from the shelters on a brilliant June morning and our house was gone. I saw part of one of my bedroom walls lying where the bus-stop used to be, a hundred yards down the road. A broken water main was shooting into the sky, and a rainbow formed above the destruction. Dust clotted and blew across the river, and I was yelled at by bystanders and a fireman. I turned to the sound of their voices and saw a loose firehouse snaking towards me. I ducked and rolled behind a heap of steaming bricks as the nozzle whipped over my head and spun back the way it had come. The hose followed, I covered my head and then the water was cut. I heard a long hiss and the hose was collapsing around me. I stood up and raised my arms. The rainbow was high, and went from the ruins to the river, and pooled its colours by the Greenwich buoys.

Mother came, hauling the two bags she had carried to the shelters, and we went to stay with Miss Joyce of Shadwell, a retired geography teacher. She lived in a house that fronted right on to the river, and I had the top room.

That room was my first bridge. I was captain and the women downstairs were crew. I organised myself and my equipment, spread my charts, issued orders and settled back in the helmsman's chair.

I set course for enemy waters, and bravely defied the U-boats. I signalled to Resistance fighters who had gathered on a lonely beach, and they rowed out to meet me. They had a wounded pilot with them, and he was transferred to my vessel. I sailed him home, once again evading the torpedoes, and his life was saved.

And I was in tropical waters, and shipping water. Sharks circled, the crew became delirious with fear. The stores were ruined; we were living on raisins and rainwater. I was sick with malaria but would not leave the bridge. Jakarta was only two days' sailing away, and a hurricane was forecast, but we would make it. We had to. The crew looked up to me, and I had given them my word. We made it.

Imagination was my friend, and protected my luck from the Blitz. Then I saw my first wrecked ship and for weeks I became dislocated, as if my best friend had died and I had seen it happen, helplessly, unable to move.

The SS *Filles de Kilimanjaro* was bombed in November, as she stood off the Limehouse Reach. She burned and sank in three hours; the river steamed and her stern stood up in the morning as if she were blaming me. I went down to look, and stood on the wharves as the salvage men went aboard, roped themselves together and climbed to the bridge deck to haul down the ensign.

It was a cold day, and sleet blew across the river and around the staggered ruins of the docks, but I wanted to strip and swim across to the *Filles de Kilimanjaro*. I knew I couldn't help or do anything at all, but I wanted to touch her. I wanted to run my fingers over her rudder and feel her rivets before she was hauled away.

Mother came down with Miss Joyce, and they wouldn't let me stay. I had to go back to Shadwell, but I looked over my shoulder all the way, and when I was in my room I stood at the window and asked the river how far to sea it went. How far it carried fresh water to the salt, and did it die somewhere?

I heard the women talking. Miss Joyce said, 'I think you should take him to the country.'

'Maybe...'

'If the bombs don't get him, I think his head will.'

'He is very imaginative. He always has been.'

'My sister's in Somerset, lives on a fruit farm. She's got three children of her own, but I'm sure she could take you. She's got plenty of room.'

'Somerset... I don't know. I think Michael would miss the river. I'll have to think about it.'

I thanked my mother. She knew how I felt. I told the river that I had never met my father, and I asked it to be him. It said 'Yes', and I believed it. The river would love and advise me.

The SS *Filles de Kilimanjaro* settled in the mud, and the tugboats hooted around her stern, waiting for the tide. A fog came down towards evening, and the river faded. Faded but never gone, always there, always mine.

5

We never went to Somerset, but when I was sixteen I went to a Thursday matinée and saw my first Elizabeth Green film. It was a light thriller called *Dangerous Brew*.

Elizabeth played Joyce, the teenage daughter of a rich businessman who wants to make her own way in the world. She packs a bag, runs away from home and gets a job as a waitress in a coffee shop.

The businessman is pacing up and down, frantic with worry, but his wife tells him not to worry. She says, 'Joyce isn't stupid,' and 'She's doing what you did when you were her age.'

'But I never had her advantages.'

'Maybe she thinks they're disadvantages...'

The father thought about that, and knew there was truth in it.

Joyce loves working in the coffee shop, and when she meets and falls in love with a customer called Danny, she feels her life is complete.

But Danny is a liar and a thief, and tries to persuade Joyce to act as lookout while he robs a drugstore. He is caught and she runs.

As I watched I was with her as she ran and hid. She couldn't believe that she had been so wrong about Danny, and as she sat on a river bridge and watched lights on the water, I wanted to go to her and hold her and tell her that I was the kind of man she needed. She could have trusted me, I would never have used her, I would never have lied to her and put her in such a fix. In close-up, her face hazed and tears filled her beautiful eyes. Her skin looked thin, and all her nerves fizzed.

My nerves fizzed... a policeman approached her... twenty-five minutes later she was home with her rich father and her mother. They sat in their sitting room and waited for the policeman to leave. I waited for an angry scene but it didn't come. Everyone had learnt a lesson except me. I went to see *Dangerous Brew* every day for a fortnight, so I could repeat entire scenes word for word, and imitate Danny's laugh perfectly.

Dangerous Brew, Lost in an Accident, Captain Gentleman, Unit 505, The Forfeit Board: these are the titles of Elizabeth Green's first five films, and I watched them all a few times, except *Unit 505*, which is a waste of time. She plays the only female member of Unit 505, a top-secret government organisation. She had to dye her hair black for that one, and spent most of the time nodding and agreeing with men in suits.

Elizabeth Green, with your cheap films and your skin like glass and your hair tumbling on to your shoulders. Your blue eyes blinking, and your mouth opening slightly. I missed you when I went to sea but grew closer to you. I invented new roles for you, and you played them better than any I had seen at the Gaumont, endlessly.

I was eighteen in 1945 when I left home and joined my first ship. Apprentice on the SS *Iris* out of Tilbury, carrying grain and sugar to Skolvig.

My mother held me in her arms and I knew what she was going to give me. Her eyes were bigger than hope or the moon in the sky. We stood together at the seamen's gate. The ship loomed behind us and the derricks swung the last loads aboard. The night was thick, and tried to swallow our words. Lights shone on the river, and all the things the river was flooded my head. Father, excuse, work, escape. 'This is yours,' she said.

'What is it?' I pretended.

'I'll show you.'

The man's leather cap was still in its brown paper bag; she took it out and brushed fluff off the peak. 'Always wear it,' she said. 'I bought it when you were born. It's lucky.' She stroked the lining and started to cry. 'You know why, don't you?'

'No.'

She said, 'You were born a special baby. You were born in your caul. Do you know what that is?'

'Sailors keep them?'

'Yes. But do you know why?'

I didn't.

She explained. Her womb, blood on her fingers, her waters not breaking, her first sight of my shrouded head, the midwife's shriek. 'Promise me, Michael,' she said, and she put it on my head. She adjusted it carefully, and stroked a curl of my hair. 'Will you?'

I didn't need to ask why. I reached up and touched her hand, and said, 'I promise.'

She kissed me.

'Always,' I said.

'Darling...'

She had never called me that. 'Mother...' I buried my head in her shoulder and breathed her scent of carbolic and coal smoke. She patted my cap and I looked at her. Deep lines creased around her eyes and mouth, and glistened with tears. She looked very tired, and for a moment I had to stay. I could not leave her under the damp stars, with the fog on the water and the drunk sailors who trailed through the gate. But the ship hooted and I turned towards the sound.

'And don't forget your mother.'

'Never.'

'Write, won't you?'

'Every day,' and I showed her a pad of paper and a blue pen I had bought specially.

'Promise again...'

'Mother...'

She took a deep breath and sprayed me with tears. 'I'm missing you already.' She gulped. 'Michael...'

'I've got to go, Mother.'

'This is the night I've waited for.'

Elizabeth Green said that to me. Who could have dreamed that?

6

I wore the man's leather cap for fifty years.

I never lost it, it was never stolen, its seams were repaired a dozen times and the peak was patched.

I became my own luck, and men I didn't know prayed to share my watch.

I retired as captain of the MV *Spanish Key*, drank half a bottle of malt whisky alone and said goodbye to my last crew in Felixstowe. I wanted to go home but I had no home to go to, no Strafford Street as I remembered it, no one who told amusing stories about my mother. I visited her grave, but the stone and the earth told me nothing. I laid some flowers on the grass, but as I was doing so I felt bad and empty. I wanted to talk to her, to ask her what I should do, but the words broke, the thoughts dissolved and I walked away with no idea at all.

I had a niece in Liverpool; I visited her but didn't recognise her, she didn't recognise me and we didn't have anything to say. She watched television during the day and stayed out all night; I packed my sea-bag and walked away again.

I was strong, I had savings. I did not want to drown in a dry place so I bought a tent and a new pair of boots. These were Italian and comfortable, and I began to voyage through the country.

One foot in front of the other and I became a story sailors tell, the one about the old captain who travels the earth looking for the comfort the ocean used to give him. He sees meaning in the shape and track of clouds, and in the cast of the sun. He stands at crossroads and can hear waves as they break a hundred miles away, and he always heads towards them. He carries a shell in his pocket, and lines his shoes with seaweed, but he will always be disappointed, he will never find what he is looking for. His hands soften, he forgets to work, he weakens and dies alone in a churchyard.

I avoided churchyards, worked casual jobs and visited every county. I never stayed long in one place, never got into a fight, never hurt anyone, never kissed a woman. Dogs liked me; they would gather at my feet if I sat in a park to eat a pie, and I would talk to them. Their owners would whistle and they'd hesitate before leaving me, but I'd wave them away, and leave alone.

I dug ditches in Lincolnshire, built a wall in Yorkshire and sawed logs in Derbyshire. In Dyfed I painted a young farmer's caravan, and played with his dog along the shore. In Norfolk I cleared shingle from a widow's garden, and spread it on her drive. I visited Scotland, and spent a month on the Clyde. I haunted the deserted docks, and watched the tides. I collected driftwood and tried to whittle animals — fish, rabbits, ducks and chickens — but I never got the hang of it.

The Clyde, Lothian and the Lammermuik Hills led me to Northumberland, where walking and working and keeping busy caught up with me. One morning I woke up with a pain in my chest and weakness in my legs; when I tried to move, I couldn't. I lay in my bag, in my tent, listened to the wind on the canvas and had no choice. I began to call for help.

I called for hours. I managed to crawl to the front flap and open it, and then I lay back with a view of the beach and the North Sea, a cruel, grey bastard of water. I shouted 'Help!' and 'Hello!', and rubbed my legs, but I couldn't get any warmth or feeling into them. I began to feel curious and detached from the world, as if I was beginning to slip away from it. I was overtaken by a light-headedness; this wasn't a drunk feeling, more like a release of pressure in my head. I cared, but I didn't care. I wanted to enjoy life but I decided to stop calling for help and lie back instead and let the cold northern air freeze me dry.

I was making myself comfortable, listening to my bones as they creaked, and I was wondering about God, prayers and missed opportunities when I heard movement outside. A timid voice said 'Hello? Is anyone there?'

'Yes!' I called. 'In here!'

I sat up, and as I did a face appeared at the front flap, a round face with spectacles and a beard. 'Hello?' it said, and was joined by another, a woman. 'Are you all right?'

Sometimes it is difficult to be civil. I wheezed deeply, and said, 'I can't move my legs.'

The woman looked at my feet, then looked at the man, and back at me. Her eyes lit up, and her mouth curled into a grotesque smile of sympathy. 'We'll call you an ambulance. Brian?'

'Sylvie?'

'Go and call an ambulance. I'll stay here.'

Brian pushed his glasses up his nose with his middle finger, and jogged away without another word.

I spent a difficult hour with Sylvie, who was one of the most talkative people I have ever met. She told me about her work for British Telecom, her dislike of children, her husband's dental practice, her home town of Oldham and the price of a cup of tea in the café they'd just visited. 'A cup of tea, you wouldn't believe it. Mrs Weggley does a mug, a mug mind, for twenty-five pence. That café; you couldn't drown a mouse in their cups.'

I wondered: could the discomfort of a slow death in a stranded tent be any worse than this as she went on and then changed the subject without a breath and told me about the many walking holidays they had enjoyed. Of course they used to go on boating holidays — narrow boats, mainly — but now it was just walking. She would ask me a question but not bother to wait for a reply. 'Are you on holiday too? This time of year is so good for holidaying, isn't it? Would you like a biscuit? Northumberland's such a surprise, don't you think?'

Brian reappeared with a red face and the news that the ambulance was on its way. He was going back to the main road, where he had promised to meet them and direct operations.

There was nothing I could do. I felt pathetic, useless and old. The ambulancemen tried to make light of the situation, cracking jokes about this and that, but I didn't join in. Some feeling was returning to my legs, the numbness was stealing away; I sat up, and watched the fields fade at the edge of town.

I couldn't remember the last time I had seen the inside of a hospital. I was carried in and put on a bed in a cubicle in out-patients. When the doctor came to see me he took my wrist, checked my pulse and remarked that men of my age should be careful when they went on camping holidays. 'The cold's more dangerous than you think,' he said. 'You don't know that it's creeping up on you, and before you know it…' He cut the air with the side of his hand.

'What?' I said. 'Before I know what?'

'You could end up not waking up.'

'Really?' I said.

'Really,' he said, then, 'I'd like to keep you in for a couple of days. Run a few tests.'

'What tests?'

'You say you couldn't feel your legs?'

I nodded.

He looked at the clipboard at the end of the bed. 'I can't see your address. Where's home?'

'My tent is my home.'

The doctor looked at me sideways, shook his head and said, 'You don't look like…' He hesitated and looked at his shoes.'… like a man of the road.'

'I'm not,' I said, and now I felt better. I swung my legs off the bed, stood up and staggered as I reached for my coat.

'But you live in a tent?'

'Yes,' I said, and I dropped the coat and had to sit down.

'In all weathers?'

'Of course,' I said, and I told him half my story.

'When was the last time you had a check-up?'

'I don't know. Five years ago? Six?'

'Okay. Okay...' He rubbed his chin and pointed to my legs. 'How do they feel?'

I lied when I told him I knew I was going to be all right, and he knew it.

'Mr Blaine,' he said, seriously, 'I'm going to admit you, if for no other reason than I think you need a rest. That's what most men your age do all the time.'

'I'm not most men,' I said, 'and I have a rest every day,' but the words sounded feeble. I was feeble. I remembered a captain I served under, Captain Beck, who refused to admit that he had to retire early, who called himself feeble and died of a broken heart in a basement flat in Liverpool.

'Admit your age,' he said.

'A couple of days?'

'That's all.'

I looked down at my legs, and tried to feel my toes. 'All right, Doctor,' I said.

The tests showed nothing but the doctor was right about having a rest, and told me to buy myself a bicycle. He told me that my feet were telling me something, and my legs too. He said, 'If I'm in as good shape when I'm your age, I'll be a happy man.'

'Happy?' I said, and I wanted to ask him what the word meant. He was an intelligent man, but there was something missing from his life. When he looked at me I think I saw a hint of envy in his eyes. His work never gave him time to reflect, his young children were tiring, his wife was tired, he hadn't been to the cinema for years.

'Yes,' he said.

There was something I wanted to say to him, something more than 'Thank you, Dr Burrell,' but I couldn't get the words out. I was never good at advice. I could only give orders.

He helped me on with my coat and waved me away from the hospital.

Roads, hedges, moors and empty barns. I owned a bicycle for a year, but it was stolen in Cornwall. I had been working for a farmer, clearing dung from his barns. I had the barns clean and the cattle came in for the winter. The farmer handed me an envelope of notes, said something regretful about my bicycle, and shook my hand.

I walked again, six miles to Blackwater, then on to St Agnes. My legs were fine. I could feel every toe. I took more sit-downs than I had before Northumberland, wore my cap all the time, and two vests. Half the body's heat loss occurs through the scalp, several thin layers of clothing are better than two thick ones — these are a couple of pieces of advice Dr Burrell gave me. I didn't disappoint him by telling him that I knew. He was in my thoughts as I reached Trevaunance Cove. I camped in sight of the broken blocks of granite that used to be a harbour and decided that he would have liked the place. The beach café was shuttered. The only visitors were surfers and old women with dogs.

It rained for days, so I sat in my tent and read about St Agnes. Reading was my hobby at sea. Novels, histories and biographies; you know, the isolation of command forces a captain to develop a solitary interest. Some carve bones, others study orchids or dream about opening a hotel in a ski resort. One used to write love songs to the navigation stars and sing them to himself in the middle of the night, and I knew the Captain Willes who taught himself Cantonese, Japanese, Vietnamese and Thai.

Reading was the only thing that ever caught me, picked me up and ran. I never bothered with it when I was a boy; my imagination was stronger than words, but when I went to sea, the work smothered thinking. Hard work, deep sleep, hard, wet work, sleep so complete that I could not remember a thing about it. Books did my imagination's work.

The first novel I read was *The Happy Return* by C. S. Forester, and I was hooked. I raced through every Hornblower I could lay my hands on, before a motorman leant me *A Tale of Two Cities*. Motorman Barton of the MV *Solea* out of Hamburg, with an oily rag in his back pocket, a grease gun in his hand and every novel Dickens had written in his cabin. Dickens, Stevenson, Conrad... name it.

As I got older, my reading followed the seasons. Romances in the summer, or travel books. Biographies through the autumn, and fat, serious novels through the winter. I would lighten up as spring approached; detective stories would climb to the top of the pile, and sometimes even an old Hornblower, like an old friend sending an unexpected letter. Other worlds, other minds and the suspension of belief; these were the antidotes to navigation and the responsibilities of my work.

In the tent, as the rain poured down. I learnt that St Agnes was a Christian virgin who refused to marry, consecrating herself to God instead. She was thirteen years old when she was executed by being stabbed in the throat, and her blood rotted the feet of her executioner. That was enough: I left the cove at the beginning of November and walked to Portreath.

Three weeks later I was on the road from Zennack to Penogan. I stopped to rest on a broken stone wall. It was a thin and watery day and the road to Port Juliet crossed the fields that dropped to the sea, but I didn't see it. I ate a cheese roll, and an apple.

I like fruit. Dr Burrell had told me to eat as much of it as I could. 'Especially oranges. You can't have too much Vitamin C.'

I scuffed the ground with my boots. I never forgot to rub dubbin into their stitching every night. I noticed a beautiful lichen on the wall, and a wren hunting spiders in the cracks. The clouds gathered above me, the first drops of rain began to fall, and a wind blew in from the sea.

I turned to watch the weather come and as it did the fields changed from pale to wild, and I saw the road's first bend. I stood up and saw more, and followed the wall to a gap, and the tumbled signpost in the verge. Thunder rumbled over the ocean, and the sun failed.

I was at sea again. I was in the Baltic, twenty, working for my steerage certificate through waves the size of cathedrals and spires. The captain was brazen and happy. As we yawed and smashed through, he yelled and took photographs of my expressions. He would say, 'There's nothing to it,' about anything.

Playing violin in a symphony orchestra. 'There's nothing to it.'

Writing *Lord Jim*. 'Nothing to it.'

He took a photograph of me and said, 'If I can do this anyone can. All you've got to do is point and press the button. There's nothing to it.' He didn't notice the sea, the screaming of the engines, the pumps racing or the buckled bow rail. He took another photograph. 'Piece of cake,' he said, as the door to the bridge wing suddenly cracked, opened and water slewed over us. 'Secure that!' he shouted.

'Sir!'

I left my position at the chart table and grabbed the door handle. As I did, the ship yawed over another wave, slewed to starboard and I slewed too, out of the door and on to the wing. I saw a bulkhead and I saw a rail; I put my arms out as I fell, banged my head against the bottom of the compass housing and slid towards the rail. I heard the captain shout my nickname, 'Lucky...', like the last word of a prayer, the ship yawed again, and I was tipped through the rail to the deck below.

As I fell I remembered dozens of things. First, take your cap off and stuff it down your shirt. Second, call your mother's name. Third, put your arms over your head. Fourth, yell. Fifth... Sixth... Seventh... I saw a lifebelt attached to the deck below me, then the ocean opening for me, then the lifebelt again and I landed next to it. I clipped my head on a cowling, tried to sit up, couldn't, sat down and was immediately picked up by a churn of water and swept towards the bows.

I heard the captain yelling again, it was my name, my name, and as I passed the bosun's cabin I saw his face at the porthole. It was trapped and white as the ship pitched me on, and my arms thrashed and I tried to grab anything I could, anything under those circumstances. I saw lights and a wall of water, and I saw a wall of sky. My head filled with salt and my mouth with terror; the water slammed over the bows, wrenched a bolt from a hatch and tossed it towards me. I saw it coming, I watched it sitting on the lip of a curl of a wave and I knew it was coming for me, I could see the glint on the edge of the steel. Stupid how you think you recognise death; I remember wondering if the captain would be angry because I had not secured that door, as the bolt flipped off the lip and shot past me. I saw it, it was an inch away from me, flying, twisting in the air, rusty at one end and shiny where it had sheared. I ducked and felt a stanchion brush my shoulder. I grabbed it, I heard the bosun's shout, the ship slewed again and I was wrenched around and creased against a ventilator. Another wall of water, another of sky, another wrench and I grabbed the stanchion with my other hand, and would not let go. I held on for a minute, waving backwards and forwards, feeling my cap against my skin, my skin against my cap, my cap doing its work, my cap warm as my mother's face, my hot cap. I took short, shallow breaths.

I saw the bosun's face again, this time ten feet away, looking around a corner, holding a roped lifebelt. Another face appeared beside him, and he shouted, 'Lucky!'

I tried to shout, but failed.

'We're going to throw this!' He held up the belt. 'We'll haul you in!' The sea broke again, the ship screamed, I yelled, 'Throw it!', and he did. It skidded down the deck and clipped my knees; as I caught it I was swept sideways, away from the stanchion to the rail. The ocean yawned beneath me, the bosun shouted, 'Do it, Lucky!', and I did. I got my arms into the belt, wrapped the ropes around my wrist and I felt the first steady tug. Then another and I was being pulled. I was losing my strength but I didn't care. I looked up and saw the captain leaning over the bridge wing. He was holding his camera, and when he saw that I was safe he took a photograph of me and called, 'Change his watch. Bosun!'

'Aye, sir.'

I never owned a camera. Maybe I should have. Maybe I have been wrong to think that I will never forget. The first time I walked the road to Port Juliet, the first time I saw the ruins, the first sight of my house; everything has blurred into one. Broken waves were crashing along its shore, the offshore stacks could not be seen, the wind picked up rocks and lobbed them on to the beach. I remember these things, but at the moment, at that moment I didn't recognise what I saw. I didn't see the ruins as a ship to guide me, or a light blazing.

I camped for three nights, then walked away. I was an hour gone before I realised I'd left the place I'd set out to find. I turned around and prayed that I hadn't dreamt the place. I began to run. I put my hand on my cap. I was thinking straight. The clouds stopped and I thought: *Enough*.

I bought the house from a man I never met, a Mr Simonswell. He lived in a London nursing home and owned property in fifteen English counties; the business was concluded through a solicitor in Zennack, Mr Parker. He was an old man with a room of files but never the right one. He smoked a pipe and never opened his windows. He had a huge nose and very spidery writing. He didn't ask me any personal questions.

7

I was on my roof when I saw the woman coming. She was walking down the road. Her hair was white like frost. I was fixing ridge tiles, bedding them in cement. While I was up there I had checked the chimney.

I crossed the roof, climbed down the ladder and whistled for Gloria. We crossed the track behind the house and stood in the shelter of the ruined barn. From here we could see the road, my house and the edge of a bank of cloud as it rolled in from the sea. Gloria looked up at me with her tongue hanging from the side of her mouth. I touched her nose and said, 'Don't make a sound.'

The woman stopped and stared towards the ruins. She turned and looked over her shoulder, and shielded her eyes, and I shielded my eyes towards her. The wind rustled the grass that grew all around, and larks rose.

She was wearing a black dress, a blue scarf and black shoes. These were unsuitable for the road. As she walked, one slipped off. She stopped and bent to put it back on. A gull dived, screeched over her head and disappeared. She waved her fist and I heard her shout. Her voice was loaded with shock and disappointment. She disappeared behind the ruins of the farmhouse then emerged again. She was holding her knee, and grumbling. She walked as far as the grass that grows above the beach, shielded her eyes again and stared towards the offshore stacks. The tide was flooding and racing to the shore. A flight of oystercatchers was crying at the ocean, and running with the breaking waves. She opened her mouth to shout, then shook her head.

She turned and walked towards my house. When she saw my tools stacked by the front door she called 'Hello?' The word was caught by the wind, flipped like a pancake and laid on the ground. A pair of chickens crossed her path, and the cat. Now she was twenty feet away, and as she stepped up to the door I recognised her.

Elizabeth Green: at that moment in the spring my heart attacked me and refused to listen. I felt a pair of hands push me from behind and lift me up. All the blood in my legs rushed to my chest, and my fingers fisted with shock. I could not help myself. My head burst. I had to close my eyes. When I opened them again you were still there but I could cope. I took a deep breath and let it out slowly.

Missing You is a great film. I remembered the first time I saw it, and the times since, and the people I took to see it. Your face, your eyes… Your face had lined but your eyes were the same, and your beautiful mouth. I had dreamt about that mouth. Once I had wished your lips on mine. My right knee began to shake. I gripped it and took another deep breath. My vision blurred. I rubbed my eyes.

Elizabeth Green stopped at my front door, touched her hair, said 'Hello?' again, and knocked. 'Is anyone there?' She pushed the door, and it swung open. She stood where she was and looked at the stuff in the hallway. There was a pair of boots and some lengths of planed wood, and a model sailing ship on a high shelf. There was the smell of dog and earth there, and the sound of a hissing fire. She took a step inside and as she did I relaxed. Gloria broke away and rushed her.

Elizabeth Green was surprised. The dog pushed her down the hall and into the kitchen, where she tripped over a basket and fell on to the mat in front of the fire. I came running, and when she saw me she put her hands to her face and screamed. The noise she could make was incredible. She was a small woman wearing a brooch that could buy Truro. I backed off, put my hands up and said, 'Gloria!' The dog backed off and went to a corner.

The scream was still echoing in my head when Elizabeth Green yelled 'Call it off!' at me.

I said nothing.

My cheek twitched.

'Are you going to just stand there?'

I didn't move.

The dog grinned and slavered.

I didn't move.

She said, 'What's the matter with you?', grabbed the top of the stove and pulled herself up. Her dress was torn. 'God!' She fingered the tear. 'Look at this!'

I took a step forward but did not offer my hand. She had come from nowhere dressed as if she were taking a stroll down a city street and she was shouting in my house. No one had ever shouted in my house, and this was the first house I had ever owned. No one had ever been in my house. The kitchen suddenly felt very small.

'Hey!'

She was yelling again.

'Is anyone there?'

When I was apprenticed, this was something one of my captains used to say. My mind would be alert but my face would be blank, my eyes dim, my arms relaxed and hanging straight down. This captain used to worry about me, he thought I was going soft, too long on watch, too young to be so long at sea, too far from land.

Elizabeth stood up, grabbed the back of a chair, pulled it out and sat down. I moved to one side, steadied myself against the wall and said, 'What are you doing?'

'Ah!' Now Elizabeth snorted and rummaged in her bag for a handkerchief. 'You talk.'

I nodded.

'But not much?'

'Enough,' I said, and, 'What are you doing here?'

'This is Port Juliet?'

I nodded.

'Oh God.'

'What's the matter? Are you lost?'

'Do I look lost?'

33

I pointed to her shoes. 'Yes.'

She waved her handkerchief at me. 'I'm not,' she said, and, 'This is it?'

'Yes.'

'There's nothing else? Just this?'

'I like it.'

'But I was expecting... I don't know. A port?'

'Were you?'

'Of course!' She yelled again, and her eyes swivelled towards the door. 'Wouldn't anyone?'

'I don't know,' I said. 'I don't meet many people.'

'You surprise me.'

'I've got Gloria.' At the sound of her name, the dog got up and stood by my side.

'Wolfhound?'

'Yes.' I rubbed her head.

'I thought so.'

'She didn't mean to jump you.'

She put out her hand and Gloria moved forward and licked it.

'So you...' I wanted to tell her I loved her. I felt that confident.

'Yes?'

I stared at her hair. It was beautiful.

'Hello?'

And her eyes were deep blue, stormy at the edges, wide, staring at me.

'What's the matter with you?'

I said, 'What do you want?'

She did not answer straight away. She looked around the kitchen, then out of the window. She could see the ruined roofs of the weavers' cottages, and hear the sea. The sun was sinking. Rooks drifted home, and gulls watched the tideline. A kettle was steaming on the stove. The fire smoked. She whispered, 'I don't believe it.'

How many things do I want to ask you? 'What?' I said.

She looked directly at me and her eyes had me and knew it. There was nothing I could do. It was unfair. I tried to tidy my hair but could not. Her lips were too red and her mouth was like a flower slowly opening. At that time she was seventy-five years old, and had been married three times. She should have died forty years before, then she could have lived for ever; you cannot carry a face like that for so long. Hair like a storm. She said, 'Do you know who I am?'

I said, '*Missing You's* one of my favourite films.'

'Is it?'

'Yes.'

She dabbed at her hair. It was very fine and light, and feathered through her fingers. 'My mother was born here.' She looked out of the window again. 'I came to see the place she wanted to leave.'

'Did you?'

'Yes.'

Once I had her photograph pinned over my berth, and another in my pocket. For years she was my woman aboard, the one I had when I was alone. I left her when I went ashore, but I always went back to her. I loved her, I wanted her, I held her face in my gripped fingers.

She said, 'How long's it been like this?'

'Like what?'

'Ruined.'

'I don't know.'

'And you're the only person here? There's no one who could tell me anything about the place? About the old days. Mother didn't tell me anything.'

'There might be someone in Zennack.' My voice slipped.

'That's where I just came from.'

I cleared my throat. 'How?'

'Cab.'

'Where is it?'

35

'I let him go.'

'Didn't he ask how you were getting back?'

'No.'

'Then how are you?'

'I'll give him a call.'

'You can't. Not from here.'

'I'm sorry?'

'I haven't got a telephone.'

'What?'

'No phone.'

She laughed. 'I don't believe you. Come on!'

I shook my head. I felt bad.

'Everyone's got a phone!'

'I haven't.'

'Please.' She was pleading, her voice trembling. 'Please, it can't be happening again…'

'What can't?'

She put her hand over her mouth, and sagged. 'Then…' she mumbled.

'Want a cup of tea?'

'Got anything stronger?'

'Whisky?'

'Never mind.' She looked in her bag again and pulled out a bottle of vodka. 'A glass?'

I fetched one.

She poured and drank. 'Okay.' She touched her lips with her fingertips. 'Okay…'

I went to the cupboard, took out a cup and saucer, and a teapot.

'Okay… What's your name?'

'Michael.'

'Michael.' She said it slowly.

'And you're Elizabeth Green.'

She nodded. 'Yeah.'

'Yes,' I said.

She narrowed her eyes. They were unforgiving.

The kettle boiled, and I spooned some tea into the pot. I poured on the water, then sat down. Elizabeth's scarf had come undone, and the top button of her dress. She did not look comfortable but she looked warm. There was colour in her cheeks.

'Tell you what...' She sat up. 'I'll pay you to give me a lift back. I'd like another look round the place, but whenever you're ready...'

'I'm sorry.'

'Don't worry.' She took some notes from her purse. 'I can pay.'

'It's not that.'

'Then what is it?'

'I haven't got a car.'

Now Elizabeth Green's jaw dropped. She stared at me and I stared back. Her hair had collapsed, and her eyes were fading. A vein in her neck stood up. I looked away.

'I don't believe this.'

I shrugged.

'No car?'

'No.'

She stood up and went to the window. She stared out. The sky was darkening, and spots of rain were flying against the plastic. 'What am I going to do?'

'I don't know.'

She turned and looked around the kitchen. There were bags of cement stacked in one corner, and the remains of a meal on the sideboard. There was a hole in the ceiling. The wind began to whistle around the door and suddenly I was struck by the state of the house. For fifty years of my life I had lived in strict order, shipshape and Bristol. Made bed, polished desk, clean bathroom, scrubbed sink. Decks washed, rust chipped and rails painted. No short-cuts. And when I was on the road

I kept my pack neat. Now I was talking to the first visitor in the first house I had owned, and the place was a mess. I was ashamed. I wanted to go outside and breathe deeply. I said, 'There's no excuse,' to myself, and her.

She shivered. 'No phone. No car. It's impossible.' She hugged herself.

'I'm sorry...'

She shook.

'You could...'

'Where's the nearest house?'

'This is the nearest house.'

She slapped her forehead. 'You call this a house?' She was yelling again. 'This is a construction site! I need a house where...'

'There's one on the road to Zennack. About three miles away.'

'You're kidding!'

'They haven't got a phone either.'

Elizabeth relaxed now, suddenly, and completely, and a strange smile crept on to her face. 'I was right,' she said. 'It is Baja. Baja again. God...'

'No,' I said. 'Port Juliet.'

'Sure,' she said, and now she took a swing at me. I caught her arm at the wrist and held it. Her fingers were inches from my face. Her knuckles were white. She wore a diamond ring. Her nails were perfect. I wanted to hold them to my face, and trace their outlines. She tried to struggle. 'Watch it,' she said. I let go quickly, and held my hands up, palms to the front.

Her eyes were popping and her tongue was darting in and out. I thought she was about to flail wildly at the mess in my kitchen and foam at the mouth. She was trying to find something to say or something else to do, but she could not. The air around us sucked, and the fire smoked again. I tried to move, but couldn't. We were standing two feet apart. She looked at her hands, then buried her face in them and howled.

8

I left Elizabeth Green staring at the fire, smoking a cigarette and drinking vodka. She stopped howling, wiped her eyes and said a short prayer to the hole in the ceiling. The plastic over the window snapped, and the wind blew down the chimney and puffed more clots of smoke into the room. She coughed.

I stood by the door and rubbed my hands. She didn't look at me. Between sips and puffs she rubbed her wrist, and took deep breaths. She was very small and lost and all I wanted to do was tell her how much she had meant to me years ago, alone in bunks in the South Atlantic and the Tasman Sea or Gulf of Guinea. Her face had been faithful to me; it had never failed me, or turned me down. Once she had been mine and she knew nothing about me. I wanted to know what that felt like, and if she ever thought about the lonesome things men had done with her picture at sea.

The wind gusted through the house, and rattled the stove. I said, 'I've got things to do,' but she didn't care about me or say anything at all. I called Gloria, and we went outside.

We walked away from the house, and up to the chicken coop. The birds were settling for the night, scratching straw and arranging themselves along their perches. I bent in to count them and they made bubbling noises at me. Their eyes were bright and healthy. I had not clipped their wings. They had laid me three eggs. I put them in my pocket and shut the door. Then I turned and went down to the beach. Gloria hung back and watched me carefully with one eye, the other on the way ahead.

I stood on the sand. The rain was heavier now, stinging through the air. I loved it. This was was my weather, my time. I swayed with the wind, I slipped into it. I saw myself at sea, deadly and young. Force Nine, Strong Gale. 'In which a full-rigged Ship would probably carry closed reefed Fore and Maintopsails, reefed Foresail and Forestaysail. Close hauled; in other words, head reaching...' I learnt these words but never knew why. Like 'The sharper the blast the sooner it is past'. I saw waves breaking over the bows of an old ship, and I saw a steady course ruined by a thief.

Aboard the SS *Pangaea* out of Hamburg bound for Guayaquil and Valparaiso with a cargo of engine parts and washing machines: this was my first voyage as a deckhand. No more apprentice, no more sleeping under the captain's companionway. I was a man. I could shave and roll a cigarette with one hand. I had seen a dead body floating in the dock, and been with a woman called Steffi from the Herbertstrasse. She was big and when she put her arms around me I got lost but didn't panic. I told myself that she was one type of port. She wore leather, and offered to turn me over and hit me with anything I wanted. A length of electric cable? A rolled-up Catholic newspaper? A canoe? Also, if I wanted, she would put vegetables and other foodstuffs up her. I thanked her but shook my head. I wanted the regular treatment, no extras. Straight, no chaser. I felt the roll of notes in my pocket and she stroked the top of my head. I was a man, and I had bought myself a new pair of boots.

Brown boots and envied. I wore them on board, and wore them for dog-watch, and when I was relieved I hung them by their laces from the end of my bunk when I went to sleep. I looked at them as I drifted off. They swayed me to sleep, and all I dreamed of was boots and Steffi armed to the teeth with a canoe and Steffi and boots and the two of us walking the Reeperbahn in boots and I was gone.

In the morning the boots were gone and the force nine was blowing. I didn't care about the weather. I asked my crewmates and searched the ship but could not find them. I went to see the mate. He was sitting with his feet on his desk, sucking a pen. He was wearing my boots. They still had the price stickers on the soles. He said, 'I didn't know you'd bought new boots.' He tossed the pen down, grinned and showed his teeth. They were black. 'We must be paying you too much.'

I stared at my boots. They were very comfortable and had strong laces. I wanted them very much. I touched my cap and the mate looked at it. He was smaller than me but had frightening eyes, dead skin and hadn't shaved for a week. He was called Clews and liked to have relations with bound animals.

I pointed at my boots and opened my mouth to say something, but no words came out. The *Pangaea* was caught broadsides, groaned, and we lurched together. I could have taken Clews's neck in my hands and killed him in that cabin, dragged him on deck and tossed him to the halibut, but I did not. I turned instead, and left the cabin.

The captain was drunk, the second mate was seasick and the crew were afraid. I was not afraid but I was disappointed. I had thought justice would be done, but Clews was wearing the boots four years later, and he lived to be eighty-nine.

As the night came, I lit an oil lamp and put it in the middle of the kitchen table. It spluttered. I adjusted the flame and lit another.

Elizabeth Green hugged her shoulders and shivered. 'Why do you live like this?'

I put some logs on the fire. 'I like it.'

'It's prehistoric.'

'You think so?'

'Yes.'

I poked the fire.

'You're not on the run?'

'No.'

'This is…' She looked around the room. '… your choice?'

I nodded.

She said, 'What a country.'

'It's my country,' but I didn't know what more to say about it. Standing on the beach had not cleared my head. Elizabeth Green had known Cary Grant, Joan Crawford, Bette Davis, Humphrey Bogart and Peter Lorre. Robert Mitchum was her friend. I had read about their relationship in a magazine. He had stood by her during the seventies and eighties, when her career had collapsed, the parts had disappeared and she had spent her time flailing. When no one returned her calls, invited her to parties, or sent a car to collect her, he had been a brother to her. When Shirley MacLaine asked him what time it was, it was because that was the only way she could get a straight answer out of him, but MacLaine never had Elizabeth's class, or her persuading eyes. I remember him, his sneer and his tattoos in *The Night of the Hunter*. '*Lord, you sure knew what you were doing when you brung me to this cell at this very time. A man with ten thousand dollars hid somewhere, and a widow in the makin.*' He was evil in that film, and a week before that moment in Port Juliet he might have taken Elizabeth Green's hand in his and said, 'Hope you find your ma's place.' Now she was sitting on the edge of my chair, shaking, with a cigarette in one hand and the vodka going down quick.

I said, 'Do you want something to eat?'

She gave me a pitying look.

I did not blame her. I cooked potatoes, beans and bacon, and gravy.

I sat down to eat at the table, cut my bacon and said, 'I've got a tractor.'

'What?'

'A tractor.'

'Does it work?'

'Sometimes.'

'God.'

'I can get to Zennack in an hour.'

'Can you?' she said.

'Not tonight, but tomorrow.' I put a piece of bacon in my mouth, and chewed. She poured herself another shot of vodka. Her nose was turning purple. 'I've got to fetch some timber.'

'Timber...' she said.

'Yes. For the house.'

She shook her head. 'There's no way I'm riding on a tractor.'

'You can't,' I said to Elizabeth Green.

'So?' she said to me.

'I can ask Dan to come and fetch you.'

'Dan?'

'The taxi.'

'Oh, yeah.' She drank. 'The cab.'

I moved some beans around my plate. They were okay, but I wished I had something to feed her. She ate food in *Missing You*. There's a scene where she has a bowl of soup and a piece of bread. She's sick with worry. Her fiancé is missing in the Middle East. She sips the soup carefully, and hardly eats any of the bread. I said, 'You'll be in Zennack by midday.'

She looked at her drink, swilled it around and said, 'Okay.'

'Until then, make yourself at home. There's a bed upstairs.' I pointed at a couch by the window. 'I'll sleep down here.'

She nodded.

'Do you want to wash?'

She sat up, touched her hair and her eyes widened. 'You've got a shower?'

'No.'

She rolled her eyes. 'But a bath?'

I shook my head. 'There's a sink at the top of the stairs. I bathe in the sea.'

'Please...'

'It's clean.'

'You're kidding,' she said, and she shook her head. 'You're not kidding...'

'No.'

43

She looked at me, through me and then stood up. She swayed, as if she were being blown, reached out and steadied herself against the wall. 'I'm tired.'

I pushed my plate across the table, picked up a lamp and said, 'I'll show you the way.'

She took a deep, heavy breath. I went first, pointing out the missing bottom stair, and telling her to watch out for nails sticking out from the wall. I stopped at the top, opened the landing cupboard, showed her the sink and said, 'I'll fetch you a towel.' She gasped, and covered her mouth with her hands. I went to the bedroom.

Elizabeth Green stood at my bedroom door while I pointed to the mattress on the floor, the piled blankets, the lumpy pillows and a cold cup of tea. I put the lamp on a chest of drawers, bent down and straightened the blankets. There was a pile of books in one corner, and a collection of sea-shells on the window sill. Planks of wood were stacked along one wall, and a couple of bricks. A sheet of plastic covered the window. It cracked in the wind. I said, 'I'm getting some glass.'

'This is bad.'

It was but there was nothing I could do. I said, 'I'll fetch that towel.'

'I've got to sleep here?'

'Yes.'

'How can I?'

'You've got no choice,' I said, and she laughed, hollow and short. The noise cut. I waited a moment, then went back downstairs.

9

I slept badly, drifting in and out of a dream about the Lyme Chicken Festival. The rain poured, and the roof creaked. All the doors in my house rattled with the wind. The sea raged along the shore, and its sound beat against the walls, and I thought that this was the only house I could ever have owned.

My couch was uncomfortable. I like to sleep in a proper bed. I heard Elizabeth Green creaking above me, and in my dozing I thought, No, she's not upstairs at all. She didn't arrive with her jewels and a bottle of vodka. I'm sleeping downstairs because I am getting old and going mad. My imagination has caught fire.

The Lyme Chicken Festival is not held any more. It has been replaced by more usual entertainments, but for decades it was a popular attraction. I was there in 1947, on leave from the MV *Maids of Cadiz*, docked in Exmouth awaiting cargo.

Early in the year, competitors for the main event would select an eight-week-old chicken from their flocks, paying particular attention to the size of the bird's wings. Separated from the flock and fed a special diet of fresh fruit, organic corn and mineral water, they were reared carefully. Their owners guarded them at night, often sleeping with them in cramped conditions.

The festival was held in April, on the beach. It started early, with the judging of the fancy chickens. Size of crop, comb, tail feathers and puffing chest were all considered, and rosettes presented. Photographs were taken, and local newspapermen licked their pencils. I was twenty years old, and had just returned from my first transatlantic. I was more man than I had ever been, with huge shoulders and massive arms.

After the judging of the fancies, chicken races were held, and competitions like 'Chicken that most looks like its owner', and 'Miss Lyme Chicken '47', but the main event was the most eagerly anticipated, and was held in the late afternoon.

A buzz went round the beach as the competitors carried their boxed birds through the crowd. They climbed on to a wooden platform and lined up. The boxes were opened and the chickens shown to the crowd. They were wearing leather harnesses. People applauded and yelled encouragement. I drank beer from the bottle.

Helium-filled balloons were brought and attached to the chickens' harnesses by three-foot lengths of twine. Then, at the drop of a flag, the birds were released.

At first they swung madly and struggled, but then they hung limply from the balloons as they floated into the sky. It was a windless day and they rose vertically. People craned to watch while the owners took out air rifles, and aimed at the balloons. At the drop of a second flag they fired. All hit the target, and as the balloons burst, the chickens began to flap.

The winner of the event was the chicken who flew the furthest, but no one had told the birds to fly in the same direction. A couple headed towards the sea, others towards the town, a few more chose the beach. One, stunned and confused, fell without opening its wings and crashed into the sand directly in front of the owners' platform. A dissatisfied groan rippled through the crowd, and a disappointed man went to collect the corpse.

The seabound chickens flew well but failed over water; as soon as it was beneath them they panicked, tried to turn and lost momentum. They dropped behind the breakwater, and a man dived in to try and save them, but they drowned.

Meanwhile, the birds that had headed towards town struggled to gain the height required to avoid a terrace of houses, but they failed. The first bounced on to a roof with a sickening thud, dislodged some tiles and slid to the pavement badly. The second glanced a chimney pot and careered into a back garden, while the third smashed through an upstairs window. Almost immediately a woman yelled and came to the window, and screamed 'You're animals!' at us below. We applauded wildly, and cheered. I drank another bottle of beer. Another cheer went up, and we turned to watch the surviving chickens' descent to the beach. One of these would be the winner.

There were three of them, neck and neck at this stage, their burst balloons flapping beneath them, their legs stretched right out. People shouted for their favourite, and began to run towards their likely landfall. There was madness in the air, and lust, and I had had enough, and turned away. I dropped my last beer bottle in a bin and caught the bus back to Exmouth, and the MV *Maids of Cadiz*.

I woke in a sweat. Sunlight was breaking the morning. The rain had passed. I sat up suddenly, and slipped off the couch. My back was sore. Elizabeth Green was in my bed. I stood up and put the kettle on the stove.

I went outside, took deep breaths, rubbed my face and the sleep from my eyes. The sea had calmed, and birds flew over the offshore stacks. I turned and looked up at the house.

I went back inside, and upstairs. I knocked on the bedroom door, and she said, 'Come in.'

I put my head round the door and said, 'Good morning.'

She was sitting up with my shaving mirror in her hand, brushing her hair.

I said, 'Would you like a cup of tea?'

She put down her brush, lifted her chin and patted the skin beneath. 'Lemon tea?'

'I haven't got…'

'… a lemon,' she said. 'Okay. Make it plain. No milk. No sugar. Weak.'

I stood and looked at her, and I allowed my heart to swim. The sunlight was muddied by the plastic over the window, and pooled like custard on the floor. Her hair shone the colour of the flesh of some fish in a market in a port in the East. I couldn't remember which port. I couldn't remember ever going up to a woman and offering her a cup of tea in the morning. 'Weak,' I said. I thought about asking her if she wanted something to eat, but Gloria barked and I went downstairs.

* * *

An hour later I was sitting on my tractor. Smoke poured from its pipe. I don't think I got a good deal when I bought it. I wasn't concentrating. Gloria sat in the link-box.

Elizabeth said, 'When will you be back?'

'In a couple of hours.'

'What time?'

'Eleven,' I said. 'Or twelve. I haven't got a watch.'

'You haven't got a watch...' Her voice trailed away. 'Stupid of me to think you'd have a watch.'

'There's a clock in the post office.'

'Is there?'

'Yes.'

'Can you tell the time?'

I ignored this remark. Gloria looked towards the road. I said, 'Make yourself at home.'

She said, 'What am I going to do?'

'I don't know. Go for a walk?' I pointed towards the point.

'A walk?'

'Yes.'

'You must be kidding.'

'No.'

She thought. 'Where?'

'There's a path along the cliff.'

She shook her head. She looked at her feet. 'I haven't got any shoes. And my clothes are...'

'Help yourself to some of mine. There's a clean pile in the bedroom.'

'Yours?' Her voice sounded distant, as if she couldn't hear it herself. She looked at my trousers. They were brown, stained with salt and earth, and hung in creases over my boots. My shirt collar was frayed to the tips, and the lining of my jacket was torn from back to front. My coat was thick, with wide lapels and a broad belt. I wasn't wearing a tie. I had let my standards slip. 'I don't think so,' she said.

Once, twice, three times, endlessly I had dreamed about Elizabeth Green arriving at my door in distress, drinking in front of my fire, warming herself back to life. You know you do, you know how being alone breeds a dream's furthest borders. Life is not a dream. Don't believe people who say it is. Life is actually happening to you.

'Please yourself,' I said.

She gave me a pitying look. I slammed the tractor into gear and headed up the road. I did not look back or raise my hand.

10

I drove slowly and allowed my mind to clear. I passed a farm where a child was fetched in from the step. A pair of cows was grazing in the field beside the road. They looked towards me. A curtain twitched in the farmhouse window, and a woman's face appeared. Gloria stood in the link-box and watched the cows. Her tail wagged and her tongue hung from the corner of her mouth like a leaf.

As we drove into Zennack more children were whisked away. Cats glided over fences and on to roofs. Mrs Boundy watched from the post office window as I steered across the square, past the pub and the pavement benches to Dunn's Builders' Yard of Zennack.

Mr Dunn came from a shack in the corner of the yard, rolling up his sleeves and licking doughnut sugar from his lips. He was a fat and bald man. His pate was covered with a light dusting of cement. He didn't care if I had murdered men or stolen women from their homes and sold them to passing slavers. If I paid his account on time or, better, cash in an unaddressed envelope, then I was his friend. 'Michael,' he said. 'Good morning. Gloria.' He patted the dog. 'Still busy?'

49

'Yes,' I said. We shook hands, and I said, 'I need some timber. Two by fours.'

'I've got short lengths I could let go cheap.'

'What are short lengths? How short?'

'Three, three and a half foot.'

'Okay.'

'I'll show you.'

We crossed the yard and went inside a low shed. Wood was stacked to the roof and cement dust columned in the light. I stood back while he pulled the timber from its racks, and laid it on the floor. He had a tape measure, and used it quickly. Gloria stood outside and stared at a child that stood by the fence. Everything was very businesslike. Mr Dunn did not ask me any personal questions.

I went to the post office and asked if Dan was in the village.

'He's gone to Plymouth,' said Mr Boundy. 'Won't be back till tomorrow morning.'

'Plymouth?'

'Yes.'

'Oh,' I said.

'You need a taxi?' I don't know if this was a question or a statement of fact. You need a taxi.

I said, 'I've got this woman at the Port. She turned up yesterday.'

He smiled and his teeth yelled at me. I took a step back. He said, 'We know.'

I looked into Mr Boundy's eyes. He was Cornish and had the dull look of men who have lived in one place so long that they think it is the only place. I have known people like this with their clenched hearts and their whispers. Mr Boundy was harmless but not to himself. He popped his tongue into his cheek. I said, 'Elizabeth Green' to him.

'*Missing You*, wasn't it?'

I nodded.

'Load of rubbish,' he said. 'Couldn't make head nor tail of it. Lost the thread completely. You know it was on telly last month?'

Missing You is a simple story. I said. 'Tomorrow morning?'

'Yes.'

'There's no one else who could…'

'Insurance,' Mr Boundy interrupted.

'What?' I could hear Mrs Boundy shuffling around in the back room.

'It's insurance, isn't it? If you're a fare-paying passenger and you have an accident, who's going to cover you?'

'What if she's not paying?'

'No one's going to do it for free.'

'I'll pay.'

Mr Boundy smiled now, and smoothed his greasy hair. He had a moustache and was about fifty years old. I knew what he was going to say before he said it, roughly. 'Desperate, are you?'

I stared at his mouth.

'You'll have to wait. Tomorrow morning. He'll be along, no worries.'

'Don't forget, will you?'

'No,' he said.

I moved from the counter to the corner of the shop where he keeps a small selection of fruit and vegetables. I looked at his scraggy carrots, bought a pound of apples and asked if he had any lemons.

'Lemons?' he said.

'Yes.'

'I think so,' and he came and found one hidden behind the bananas. 'We always keep a few.' He wrapped it. 'You haven't bought one before, have you?' and I knew he was going to ask why, but I gave him a hard stare, the captain's look, and he didn't say anything else.

I left the post office and as I crossed the square to the tractor, Mrs Bell came from her guest house and raised her hand.

51

'Michael!' she called, and this time there was no way to avoid her. She waved and I waved back. The sun was weak in the sky, and not very warm. She was wearing a blue apron over a floral dress, and a woollen hat. I went to meet her.

Mrs Bell's eyes were too big for me, too moist and wanting. She doesn't believe any of the stories about me, even though I insisted that most of them could be true. I stayed in her guest house for a few nights in the winter, while I was buying my house. She fed me huge breakfasts, offered me exclusive use of the top bathroom and gave me the biggest bed in the place. She told me that I was to make her house my house. I tried to tell her that I couldn't do that but she insisted. I didn't want to argue, so I thanked her though I didn't mean it. She owns a dog called Vauxhall, a retired greyhound.

I told her my story and she took me into her confidence by telling me her husband's story. He had worked as a rigger for the Electricity Board. One day he had been working on a feeder line from Penzance to St Ives. He was harnessed up all right, but as he was moving his braking clip from one spar to the next, he lost his grip. He was one hundred and twenty feet up. He tried to find a footing, slipped, shouted and dropped ten feet. Now he was balanced on a crossbeam, clear air behind, struts to the front. He tried for another grip but twisted, tipped sideways and fell another ten. Here the beams were broader and the pylon wider. One of his harness clips clattered on to his head and began to play out beneath him. He grabbed it, clipped on, fell again and hung in mid-air with nothing between him and the ground. The harness held but he was being strangled one hundred feet up. 'Help...' he wheezed to a man twenty feet below, who looked up, yelled to a third and started to climb. Mr Bell was unconscious on arrival at hospital, in April 1965, and remained in a coma for six weeks.

When he awoke on a sunny June day, Mr Bell announced to Mrs Bell that he had had a revelation. Evil in this world was being channelled into homes down electricity cables, and was seeping into people through radios, light-bulbs, twin-tub washing machines and irons. It was his mission to spread this news. He got up, dressed quickly and discharged himself from hospital.

The doctors explained that his condition was caused by lack of oxygen to the brain, and after a series of adventures in St Austell and Indian Queens, Mr Bell was committed to a hospital where he died three years later, having revised his revelation to include water. 'Washing is the worst thing you can do to yourself,' was one of the last things he said to Mrs Bell. She mourned for six months then sold their place in St Austell and bought the house in Zennack. She had always wanted to do bed and breakfast. 'Looking after people. Giving them a good breakfast. That's what counts.'

'It's one of the things.'

'I knew a man like you before,' Mrs Bell said to me. I didn't ask where. 'I could trust him. You can't trust anyone in this village. That's what I miss.' She lowered her voice. 'Confidences.' She reached out and touched my sleeve, and gave me a longer look than she had to. 'I expect on board a ship you had to be careful what you said.'

I said that you did.

'And I miss just sitting, just enjoying someone else's company. Not having to say anything…'

'I know what you mean,' I said, and at that moment I knew I'd said the wrong thing. I gave her the wrong signals, but she smiled and nodded as if I had the nicest face and had said the wisest thing.

Now she offered me a cup of tea. She had the kettle on. I followed her inside. Gloria sat by the front gate. Vauxhall watched her from the doorstep, then lay down and went to sleep.

I put my shopping on the kitchen table, sat down and waited for her to join me with the teapot. It was a comfortable scene. Mrs Bell took her apron off before sitting down. She didn't have pierced ears or a television but her skin was very pale, and her hair was dark. She had the look of a gypsy fortune-teller who gave up telling fortunes years ago, innocent eyes broken at the corners. She wore a little rouge on her face and her wedding ring on her right hand. 'So…' she said to me, and I knew what she meant.

'Elizabeth Green's at my house,' I said.

'At your house?' Mrs Bell knows what it's like at Port Juliet. 'She stayed the night?'

'Yes.'

'My God,' she said. 'In your house?'

'Yes.'

'But it's…'

'I know,' I said.

'Is she okay?' She lowered her eyes and coughed. 'What I mean to say is…'

'I know what you mean,' I said, and I smiled. 'She'll survive. I'm here to fetch the taxi for her.'

'Oh,' said Mrs Bell, and she poured the tea and told me all she knew.

Elizabeth Green was in England for the European premiere of her new film, *Raintown*. That had been last week, and now she had taken a few days off before flying back home to America.

She had appeared in Zennack two days ago. She'd taken a cab from Penzance. She booked into Mrs Bell's and did nothing but complain. First the bed was too small, then it was too high, and then the room was too noisy. When she said the bathroom was dirty Mrs Bell was indignant, told her that none of her previous guests had complained and went to make herself a cup of tea. 'I've never been so insulted,' said Mrs Bell.

'Her mother was born in Port Juliet.'

'That seems unlikely.' I don't think Mrs Bell had spent her whole life in Cornwall.

'I think it's true.'

She huffed, and poured herself another cup. 'You could eat off my taps,' she said.

'Of course you could,' I said, and I told her about the state of my house, and how ashamed I'd felt.

'Have you seen any of her films?'

'I don't think I missed one. Whenever I was in port I went to the cinema.'

'I haven't been for ages.'

'There's a cinema in Truro,' I said. 'We could go one day.'

She touched her hair and looked at her cup of tea. 'Could we?'

'Of course.'

'I'm not sure,' she said quietly. 'I don't think it would be a very good idea.'

'Why not?'

'Because...' she started, and then she coughed noisily and said, 'And the phone never stopped. In the end I had to take it off the hook.'

'When?'

'When that woman was here. I don't know. Someone from London, and then there was an American. I overheard her talking; I think she was expecting Port Juliet to be more than what it is, but I wasn't going to set her right. I thought, serves you right, treating me like this.'

'I'm sorry.'

'And she turned her nose up at my breakfasts. That was the last straw.'

'She's got very little consideration.'

'You can say that again,' said Mrs Bell, and she stood up, tapped the table-top with the tips of her fingers and went to rinse her cup.

11

When I returned to Port Juliet, Elizabeth had her hair tied back in a bun. I told her that the cab was in Plymouth. 'Where's Plymouth?'

'East. About a hundred miles.'

'So he's not coming till tomorrow?'

'No.'

'And he's the only cab in town?'

'Yes.'

'And you didn't phone for another?'

'No.'

'Why not?'

I said, 'I don't know.'

She narrowed her eyes and gave me a hard look, said, 'You don't know...' slowly, took a deep breath, turned away and looked back towards the sea. 'Tomorrow?'

'Yes.'

'So I've got to stay another night.' Her voice trailed away like vapour, blowing into lowering clouds, failing.

I took a step towards the house and said, 'Did you have a walk?'

She looked at me again, quickly, as if she was surprised to find me still there, and she said, 'Yeah.' She nodded towards the point and then she smiled at me for the first time. You know the one, the one from *Missing You* and *The Forfeit Board* and even *Unit 505*. There are dimples in her cheeks and her teeth are bright. Her head is tipped to one side and even her hair smiles. 'I went that way,' and she pointed. She looked down at her dress and her smile faded, and the hard face returned. She brushed at some dirt, then looked at her hands and winced. 'I fell over,' she said.

'Are you okay?'

'Who cares?'

'Don't you?'

'What's the point?' She looked around, opened her arms to the scene and said, 'It's such a goddamn let-down. A disappointment. Disappointment follows me.'

'Disappointment?'

'I had a picture in my head of this place. Sure, it's my fault. I had some Hollywood idea of England. People on bicycles, cheery men waving goodbye to their wives, children walking dogs.' She slapped her forehead. 'I can be very stupid.'

'No,' I said, uselessly.

She glared at me, and I waited for her to shout. I saw anger cruising behind her eyes, and then I saw her teeth. 'I...' she repeated, 'can be very stupid. Believe me. And when I say believe me, you'd better.'

'Or what?' I said. 'What are you going to do? Self-pity doesn't suit you, so maybe you should...'

'Self-pity!' She exploded. Her arms went up and down like flags up poles, and she struggled with the words she wanted to use. 'You talk to me about self-pity? You?' She jabbed a finger in my chest.

'You can make a disappointment out of anything.'

'And save your homilies for someone else.' Her face was flushed with blood.

'Okay,' I said, and I turned away, and walked past the house, up the path to the garden. At that moment I had had enough. My carrots needed me, and I was too old to argue about pointless things.

She shouted, 'Where are you going?'

I raised my hand, dropped my head and said nothing. You take some abuse, you do what you can, you seek solace in a vegetable. Disappointment is a fleeting thing, and you should learn to chase it away.

Tell me about disappointment, tell me about failure, tell me about longing. Take off your shoes, put your feet up and talk.

An hour later we sat together in the house, and I made a pot of tea. She tried to apologise for shouting, for being ungrateful. 'You had your reasons. I've been disappointed.

I understand.'

'Thanks.'

'Elizabeth Green in my house. I'll forgive her anything.'

'Sure,' she said. 'You can forgive the woman you think I am, but me. The real me?'

'Maybe.'

'Try me.'

'Okay. Tell me about Baja.'

'Baja…' she said.

'Yes.'

She lit a cigarette, and sighed the smoke at the ceiling. 'This happened to me before. Ten years ago…' Her voice trailed away. 'In 1965. After my last movie, the last one before the new one…'

'*Red Sun on the Sea*?'

'Yeah. How did you know?'

I shrugged.

'You saw it?'

'Yes.'

She laughed. 'Yeah. *Red Sun on the Sea*. God. The things I've done.'

'Why?' I made the tea.

'And the questions get bigger…' She laughed.

'I'm sorry…'

'This happened to me then. In Baja…'

'What?'

'I was stranded for a couple of days, but I got to like it. I felt that today.' She paused and took a thoughtful drag on her cigarette. 'I was almost… I was almost getting to like this place. Walking and everything. The sea, the cliffs. Those goddamn birds. Even them. Gulls, right?'

I nodded.

'It is beautiful here.'

'That's good. Isn't it?'

'Maybe. Lost days, days without names. Minutes that last hours. But then…'

'Yes?'

She didn't know.

Lost days are made by instinct. Minutes that last hours and wedge in your memory like a note. Or a scent. White flowers and wood bark blended and sealed in a beautiful bottle and hidden in a hole. Here's the hole and here's twenty cents. Go to the store and buy yourself some sweets. Go to Baja and buy yourself a memory that hibernates for thirty years and wakes to remind you that all truths are not self-evident. All truths are elemental.

I said, 'I bought a lemon.'

'Did you?'

'For your tea?' I poured it.

'Oh. Yes,' and she said, 'You didn't have to.'

'No, I didn't. But I did. How do you like it?'

'Just a slice.'

'Okay,' and I cut a slice.

She said she sat at the point, watched the sea for hours and thought about her mother. She hadn't thought about her for years, not properly, not really thinking, not imagining what it was like living in a place like this. 'She was eighteen when she left, pregnant, widowed. My father was shell-shocked.' She held up her glass. 'Came back from the war, slept with Mother, drank a bottle of whisky, fell in the sea and drowned before I could meet him. In 1919 my mother left this place. She never said much about it, and it was never good.'

I managed, 'You've come a long way.'

'From Baja…'

'What happened there?'

'I almost stayed,' she said, and I thought *Stay here* but I did not say it. I let the thought hang in the air, hoping that she would sense it, but I don't think she did.

Her clothes were a mess. I offered some of mine again and she said, 'What are you? Two hundred and twenty? I'm one-thirty.'

'There's some stuff I shrank in the wash. And I've got a spare belt.'

She looked down at her dress and brushed at a patch of mud.

I went upstairs and fetched a pair of trousers, a shirt, a pullover and a belt. I put them on the kitchen table. 'They're clean,' I said.

She looked at me. 'What can I say?' she said. 'I give you a hard time and you give me your bed and your clothes. And a cup of tea.'

'Forget it.'

'What can I do?'

'Change,' I said, and I called Gloria and we went outside, past the ruins and down to the beach.

The sea was calm, clouds were high and racing. I smelt spring in the air, warmth, and the echo of a fast passage from Tilbury to Copenhagen across the smoothest North Sea I had ever sailed, and two nights in the city. An echo of spring at sea, carried to me in Cornwall like a piece torn from an old newspaper fluttering down a street.

You never met a woman like Jytte. We met in a pastry shop. She spoke beautiful English and offered to strop my bottom while singing choice passages from Hans Christian Andersen's fairy tales to any tune I wanted. I told her that I would be happy with the basic affair but she insisted on singing anyway, and I didn't mind.

Jytte was the first woman I wanted to marry. I was twenty-five and I didn't care what she had done or how many unusual tricks she could play with her fingers; I wanted to live with her for ever. I could work in the docks, we could live in a flat over a pastry shop, we could take a daily stroll to the Little Mermaid, she could get as fat and old as she wanted. Jytte. She had more moles on her body than any woman I ever met; her skin was like the night sky in reverse. Once I tried to count those moles but gave up after a hundred, and I'd only done her shoulders and her back. 'Jytte,' I said to her, 'I want to marry you.'

'You are such a young boy,' she said, 'and I am very happy in Copenhagen.'

'I'll live here too.'

'But you are a sailor. You cannot do that.'

When I was twenty-five I didn't know that this was true. She pointed to my leather cap and said, 'Why do you always wear it in bed?'

I shook my head.

'Because you are a sailor.' She took it off my head and held it to her chest. I didn't like her doing that and she knew it, and wagged a finger at me. 'Marry you?' she said. 'I think we can do better things together than get married.'

'Only if you give my cap back.'

She felt its lining. 'I know this cap,' she said. 'The sailor's cap.'

'My mother gave it to me,' I said.

'And sewed it?'

'Yes.'

'You won't lose it.'

'I know.'

'Lose me instead.'

Elizabeth wore my old clothes but did not look lost in them, or less beautiful. Check shirt and brown trousers rolled up to her ankles. I think she could make any clothes look good, with a tuck there and a knotted corner here. I had bought a bottle of vodka in Zennack. I poured two glasses and raised mine to her. 'You look good.'

'Thanks.'

We drank slowly, and as we did she said, 'Have you got kids?'

'I don't think so.'

'What the hell does that mean?'

'I haven't got any kids. You?'

'Yeah, one.' She drank. 'Jacob. God knows what I did to deserve him. Don't believe it when people say you can't help but love your kids.' She drank some more. 'This is good vodka…'

'You must love him.'

'There you go. He loves me, but then he can't afford not to.'

I said, 'What do you mean?'

'He's the laziest man who ever lived, but he's got a hell of a lifestyle.' She lit a cigarette. 'If you know what I mean.'

'No, I don't.'

She waved her hand in the air. 'You don't want to, Michael.' She blew out smoke and looked around the kitchen, sniffed her sleeve and patted Gloria. 'This place would give him a heart attack.' She laughed and held up her glass. 'If he could see me now.' She drank. 'He doesn't like dirt.'

'Nor do I,' I said, 'but there's dirt you can see and dirt you can't. Better to see it, then you know where it is.'

'Crazy…'

'True.'

'And true, yes.' She finished her glass and poured another. 'He wouldn't understand that. Not that he understands anything.'

'Nothing?'

'This is a man who thought Pakistan was in Africa. I suppose it's my fault. I should have spent more time with him when he was a kid, and I should have learnt to say no. You can't buy off your guilt, can you?'

I said, 'No.'

She smiled and blew smoke in a thin stream, away from me towards the door. I don't like cigarettes but she knew how to smoke one. She held it like she was in love, and sucked it like she meant it. 'Sometimes I think like a movie. What do you think like?'

'Sorry?'

'You know the game?'

'No.'

'You've got to be honest. What's the thing you relate to out of all the things in the world? You know: it could be a bottle of whisky, a place, a movie, some music. Sometimes I feel like "Three Coins in the Fountain".'

'The song?'

'Yes.'

'I've never felt like a song.'

'What, then?'

'I can't think.'

'A place? Anywhere...'

I stroked the rim of my glass, swirled the vodka and said, 'Barcelona. Sometimes I feel like Barcelona.'

'Spain?'

'Catalonia.'

'Why?'

'I don't know.'

'You've got to be honest. There's no point playing the game if you're not.'

'I don't like games.'

'Barcelona?'

'Have you ever been there?'

'No.'

'It's beautiful.'

'Beautiful women too?'

'There's this park with views of the city and the ocean. Fountains, benches, places where you can get a drink. And the houses run down to the waterfront. They've got balconies, hanging baskets of flowers...'

'Why do you feel like Barcelona, Michael?'

'Because I like it?'

'No questions as answers allowed.'

'Because I like the sound of the word. Bar... cell... ona...'

'And that's a cop-out.'

'Okay,' I said. 'Why do you think like a film?'

'Sometimes...'

'Why?'

'Because sometimes I think that nothing I do is real. Every time something happens to me, I think I'm in a scene from a movie that hasn't been made yet. And I can't help thinking that everybody's watching me. As if they were at the cinema.'

'What did you do today?'

'Went for a walk. You know that.'

'And it wasn't real?'

'Not really.'

'You're happier than you were yesterday.'

'I was shocked yesterday.' She looked around the kitchen.

'I was expecting more than this. If anyone had told me I'd be spending a couple of nights in a...' She stopped.

'Say it.'

'No.'

'Baja?' I said.

She looked at the fire, and at her drink. 'What more could I want?'

'A bath?'

'Oh yes,' she said.

'The sea's warmer than than you'd think. And once you're in...'

'Don't tempt me.'

'I wouldn't dare.'

'And what does that mean?'

64

'Nothing.'

'God! I hate that! It's the worst!' She spilt some vodka but didn't notice. 'Nothing! How can something you say mean nothing? That's the kind of thing Jacob says...' Her eyes widened. '... when all the time he's scheming, or she's scheming or they're scheming together.'

I thought I might say that I had followed her career for years and that I had loved her, and some days I had thought about her all the time. I had wondered what she was doing and wondered, if I wrote to her, would the letter reach her? Would she have read it and thought about me at all? I wanted to repeat that *Missing You* was one of my favourite films, but I didn't want to bore her, I just wanted to say it again and if she wanted I wouldn't mention it again. Instead, I said, 'I don't like to tempt people.'

'Why not?'

'Temptation leads to trouble.'

She snorted. 'You believe that?'

'Yes.'

'Bullshit.'

'And you know what trouble leads to?'

'No, Michael. What does trouble lead to?'

I looked away and swimming images of Barcelona came, flowers trailing from a balcony, an open window, curtains blowing in a warm breeze.

'Michael?'

'Yes?'

'Trouble?'

Now I narrowed my eyes and I felt my face harden. Deep lines on my forehead, and across my cheeks. 'Don't ask me about trouble.'

'Is that why you're here?'

'No.'

'I knew it. You are on the run.'

'No.'

'This is your choice?'

'Yes.'

'I don't believe it.'

'But you just asked me what more anyone could want.'

'I was feeling dreamy.'

'This isn't a dream.'

'So why are you here?'

'Why. It's all you ever ask.'

'I'm an American.'

I told her that I used to be in the merchant navy. 'I was a captain.'

'No kidding. I went out with a sea captain. God...' Her eyes drifted, and clouds shaped behind them. 'A long time ago — 1970...'

Elizabeth Green's career had collapsed in the seventies. I remember that from the magazine article. It had been one man after another, and the chase for roles in films that would never be made. The chase for a bottle of whisky. Money going down the drain. Friends forgetting to send invitations. Refusing to look in mirrors. A sandwich for lunch, a whole day in bed.

'... 1970,' she whispered, then snapped back with, 'How did you end up here?'

'When I retired I didn't have anywhere to go. I hadn't made any plans, I thought the future would sort itself out and it didn't. So I went looking for one, and this is what I found.'

'Don't you miss the sea?'

'It's outside...'

'No. Being on it. The people, sailing...'

'Sometimes.'

'You don't get lonely?'

'I've got Gloria.'

'A dog?'

'And the cat.'

She laughed.

'Animals don't let you down.'

'But they can't talk.'

'That doesn't matter. There're better things to do than talk.'

'That's true,' she said, and she caught my look for a moment, held it and turned away. The dog lay down and snuffled into a dream. I poured myself another drink, a large one, and she lit another cigarette. The cat stood up, stretched and lay down again. The tobacco smoke rose in my kitchen, spewed over the lamps and layered itself beneath the ceiling. I closed my eyes and listened to the plastic rustle over the window, and the ocean as it spilled along the shore.

12

The sailor thinks he will never meet another woman like Jytte and then he meets Marianne who was born on Skopelos but moved to the mainland. She hated prunes. Her face pleaded, and every look she gave me I kept for ever. She had black eyes and long fingers. How many looks and how many women? How far does one man have to travel before he ends in the arms of one he never stopped wanting? I think about Marianne now and can see her face, but I have to concentrate if I want to separate it from other faces. I have to catch it, hold it, remember some port in some country some year when I was drinking too much and picking fights with locals. My mother had just died and I was about to apply for compassionate leave, and I clutched the man's leather cap over my heart and wished myself beside her. I wanted to feel the last warmth leave her body, and hear the last breath; I had disappointed her. I wanted to tell her that I thought about her every day, and I wanted to watch her eyes follow a single cloud and close on a sunset; I had failed. I wanted the world to acknowledge her but it didn't; it coughed like it always does on lonely people.

I'm with Marianne. We're lying in bed. She doesn't know it, but the violin we can hear is playing a lament for my mother's soul. The music floats over the waterfront and it's stronger than fate, but not luck. I hang my cap on the bedpost because that's what she wants me to do, and though I always wear it in bed with a woman I cannot say no. She runs her fingers through my hair and down my chin. I've shaved for her.

'Marianne…' I say, but she puts a finger to my lips. She tips her head back and throws her hair over her shoulder. It's long and brown. Her curtains billow, and the scents of jasmine and rosemary float in the air. A bottle of wine sits on the bedside table, and a vase of flowers. Her room has a balcony. I get up, wrap a towel around my waist and go to watch the street below, and the ships along the quay. I turn to look at Marianne, who has laid on her stomach and closed her eyes. Her left leg is pulled up, and her hands stroke the sheets. I am overcome with grief, and cannot make love.

'Cry, darling. Cry for me.'

I want to stay with Marianne but I'd prefer to sail to Tilbury with a cargo of lumber and olives. That's what she says. I cannot argue, for she is not the love of my life. I cannot tell her about my mother. I go back to bed, turn my face away from hers, and she holds on to me. We lie like that and she sleeps. I can feel her body heaving through the night, sighing and turning for someone else, mumbling another man's name in a language I don't understand. The moon sets. We're in trade, and it suits us both.

I woke early. The sun rose, birds started their singing. I left the house, walked up to the vegetable garden and sat down. My early potatoes were showing, and a row of broad beans. I had raked and flattened an onion bed, and sown cabbage. I had bought a vegetable handbook, and learnt about the planting distances, and how you must protect your seeds from pests and disease.

I poked the soil with my boots. Back-lit clouds hung like dusters in the sky. The sea was calm. The tide ebbed. The garden was protected on three sides by a high stone wall I had repaired.

We ate breakfast slowly.

'I live by the ocean. It's a new house. I only bought it last year. First real money I've had for thirty years. Would you believe it?' Elizabeth Green was still in my house. I pinched myself. She had brushed her hair. I sat so I could watch the light through the plastic shine on it. 'I've got these picture windows. You can sit in the house and it's like you're on the beach.'

'Where?'

'Malibu. It's beautiful.'

'I've seen San Francisco. That was beautiful — '51, '53, twice in '56...'

'You remember dates?'

'Yes.'

'Names and faces?'

'Sometimes.'

'So do I,' she said, and she lit her first cigarette of the day.

'You remember what you were doing in, say, the spring of 1950?'

'April 1950... I was out of Liverpool bound for Valletta, Alexandria. The Levant. I got lost in Beirut, ended up sleeping in a bar.' I remembered the place. 'It was owned by a French woman. Sylvia. She was old enough to be my mother.'

'Did you sleep with her?'

'No.'

She blew smoke out as she said, 'I got married in 1950.'

'1950...' I said.

'Divorced six months later.'

'Who was he?'

'What was he,' she said. 'That's what you should ask. He was Ray Lebox. Died last year. He was a lawyer.' She slapped her forehead. 'God! I should have known but you know how it

69

is when you're young. When you think you've got everything. He beat me up on our honeymoon night, stayed long enough to give me Jacob, then left.'

'Bastard.'

She shrugged. 'It was over before we kissed. Serves me right for not asking the right things. The only answer I got was to the question I never asked. He was the first person to tell me my career was over. Thirty years old, dead in the water. I didn't believe him. I reminded him about *Missing You* and he told me: "That was six years ago. What've you done since then?" I told him I'd made a film a year since then. "But can you remember anything about them?" ' Her voice dropped, and she asked me, 'Can you?'

'*Mercy Cure*,' I said.

She laughed, bitterly. 'Sure. *Mercy Cure*. That's what that movie needed.'

'It wasn't so bad.'

'Don't lie to me, Michael,' and her face hardened. 'I can tell.' Her lips thinned, and her eyes. 'I used to be very gullible. Still am, sometimes. Dumb,' she said, curling the word around her mouth. She leaned towards me so her face was very close to mine. 'You won't take advantage of me, will you, Michael?'

'I don't think I'm going to get the chance, am I? Dan'll be here soon.'

'Dan?'

'The taxi.'

'Oh, yeah,' she said, and she held her mouth open, and I waited for her to say something else, something to give me hope, but she didn't. She looked at the couch I had slept on, and the dog on the floor, and then turned away as the sound of the waves along the shore broke the silence.

The morning grew warm and still, and the tide flooded the beach. I had work to do in the garden. I left Elizabeth sitting in the kitchen with a cup of strong coffee and a cigarette.

I was sitting on the wall, rubbing some warmth into my knees, when Dan drove down the road and sounded his horn. I went to the bottom of the garden and waved to him, and waited for Elizabeth to appear, but she didn't. I shouted, 'She's in the kitchen,' and pointed at the house. Dan climbed out of his car, raised a hand and slouched inside. Gloria ran towards him. I called her back and we walked down together.

Elizabeth was not in the kitchen. I looked round the rest of the house but she was not there. 'Maybe she's down on the beach,' I said.

Dan looked half asleep. We walked down to the beach. I said, 'How was Plymouth?'

'How did you know I was in Plymouth?'

'Mr Boundy told me.'

'Boundy,' he muttered.

'Yes.'

'Boundy's full of crap.'

I laughed but Dan didn't. He was a thin man, young, with a gaunt face and dark, slicked hair. He smoked and chewed gum at the same time, and walked with his free hand in his pocket. When we stood on the sand he looked as though he did not belong there. He was wearing a black jacket, a white T-shirt, blue jeans and leather boots. He stared blankly at the sea and the offshore stacks, and didn't move when I suddenly yelled, 'Elizabeth!'

Gloria barked, I shouted again and then walked back to the ruins, and checked the weavers' cottages. I called her name again but she did not appear. As I was wandering around the remains of the old farmhouse, Dan joined me and said, 'I've got another fare at twelve.' He tapped his watch and scratched his cheek. His skin was pale, almost translucent, and when he coughed I thought he'd burst. The dark and troubled soul of

71

cab drivers… He struggled to light another cigarette, scratched his head and threw a nervous glance at the sky. He watched a cloud, and as it shaped over him, puffing and splitting in the stratospheric winds, despair drifted across his eyes. He looked at his boots. They were scuffed and dirty. He turned towards me, and for a moment I thought he was going to say something important. He looked as though he was about to snap with grief and a deep longing. I could taste the feeling in the air between us, salty like a memory I had of a similar longing. A cathedral of rage in my head, with blackened windows and a red roof. Overlooked on all sides, dripping with storm water, twisted with faded ivy. I said, 'I'll check the house again.'

'Okay.' He looked at the smouldering tip of his cigarette. 'I'll be in the car.'

She wasn't in the house, but I found her purse on the side-board. I picked it up and held it to my nose, put it back and went outside. I shouted her name one more time. Gloria lay down. I went to the cab and said, 'Sorry. I don't know where she's gone.'

'I've got to go.'

'Here,' I said, and I gave him a tenner.

'Thanks.' His voice was drifting. He took the money and slipped it into a purse on the dashboard.

'I'll be in Zennack this afternoon,' he said, and he drove away. I stood and watched him go, then whistled for Gloria.

We searched the ruins again, and the beach, but there was no sign of her. I took the cliff path and started to walk towards the point. The dog ran ahead. The wind was strengthening. The sea swelled towards the rocks. I was afraid. We hadn't said goodbye.

I never said goodbye to my mother. She had died in the front room of a downstairs flat I never slept in. I still see her there, alone in an armchair with a blanket covering her knees, staring through a gap in the curtain at a child riding past on a bicycle, and then, nothing. No hand to hold, no one to rush into the street wailing. Dust settling on her ornaments, and on the remains of her last meal. Her cat sitting outside, wailing at the back door. She sat dead for twenty-four hours until the milkman called the police. A few neighbours gathered to watch her body carried from the flat, and they whispered that it was a shame and a pity. She had kept herself to herself but they thought she hadn't meant it to be that way. She had a son, but none of them had ever seen me.

I was guilty. I had neglected her and never said goodbye. I was not the sort of child a mother wished for, and I was ashamed.

The funeral was delayed for my return, and afterwards I signed off for a month, and lived in the flat. I wanted to hide and lose my own face. I didn't want to spend any time with a whore. I didn't move my mother's things or clean the house. I lived with the curtains drawn, ate cold food and only went out at night. I drank in the Dock and Chain, where a man can sit undisturbed. During the day I read.

I thought I was paying penance for my neglect, but when I joined ship again I couldn't concentrate on my work, on watch or on my navigation exams. I hadn't said goodbye and I never would, I hadn't told her that I always wore the cap, even in bed. I hadn't asked her if she'd ever heard from my father. I had failed her, and hadn't understood that I was needed.

I paid the price. I failed my exams. I began to lose faith in myself. I wore shirts with frayed collars and holed trousers. I told myself that I had done to my mother what my father had done to her. At Rotterdam and Antwerp, Valencia and Salerno I stayed aboard, locked myself in my cabin and left the bars and women to the other men. I didn't want to leave another woman in my life. I read Russian novels about snow and balls and suicide until my eyes bled, and I went back for more. I wrote letters to my mother, set matches to them and dropped them from my porthole. I leant out to watch the flames tumble and hiss in the dock. I drank whisky alone, and only spoke when I was spoken to.

Halfway to the point there is a shallow crease in the land, and a fork in the path that leads to the place where I bathe. I stopped for a moment, then followed the way through a thicket of blown scrub and on to a narrow track. This wound down, bending back on itself until it reached a narrow shingle beach. The bathing place is at the far end, sheltered by a semicircle of rocks, protected from the swell by the point. I stepped on to the beach and called, 'Elizabeth!' There was no reply. Then I saw her in the sea, swimming out from behind the rocks, and my heart leapt in my chest, and I felt the hands pushing me again. The sun shone on her hair. She waved.

'Hey!' I yelled, and Gloria barked.

Elizabeth swam towards us and shouted, 'This is great! Come on in!'

I touched my cap. 'You missed your cab!'

'Screw the cab! I'm having fun!' And she swam back the way she'd come, and disappeared behind the rocks.

I sat down on the beach and watched the swell break over the stacks. Gulls flocked over them, screaming and wailing at their chicks, diving at each other and the sea. They are one of the pests I have to look out for in the garden. They will come for worms in freshly dug soil, and worms are the gardener's friend. I have strung cotton over some of the beds, and this discourages them.

I was thinking about an old captain who kept window boxes on board his ship, and grew fresh lettuce and radish in all weathers, when Elizabeth emerged from the water and climbed on to the rocks. She was about fifty yards away, naked. She shouted, 'Don't look!' I saw her back, she grabbed a towel, I looked at the stacks and the gulls. 'I'm watching you!' she called.

I stood up and said, 'I'll wait for you on the path.'

'You stay where you are!'

I sat down again, and waited.

I told her that the cab would be in Zennack that afternoon but she pretended not to hear, and told me that she hadn't swum in the sea for years, but she'd felt so dirty she had to, and now she had she was glad. 'I've never had a bath like that.'

We were sitting outside, drinking. A single lark rose, crazed by singing. A pair of chickens came and pecked around our feet. She said, 'My mother kept chickens.' She laughed. 'In New York!'

'When?'

'The thirties. They lived in the back yard. She left them when we moved west, but she never forgot them. I don't think Mother ever forgot anything.'

'Why did you move?'

'I don't know. Something bad happened, a man, I think. I don't remember much. I was very young. I think she gave the chickens to some Greeks in the street. Greeks do good things with eggs.'

'I know.'

'And chicken. Do you eat yours?'

'Ssh!' I shook my head. 'Not in front of them.'

'Sorry,' she said, and that was the first time she said that to me.

We stood up and walked up to the vegetable garden, and she asked if I'd seen *The Grapes of Wrath*.

'Yes. And I read the book. "The dawn came, but no day." '

'You read the book? Amazing...'

'What's amazing about it?'

She shook her head. 'Steinbeck got it right. I saw those things. Farms drowned in dirt, people mad with thirst.' She looked at the sky. 'Some days the sun never shone, the dust blocked it out. One place we stopped I saw a dog eating an arm. A man's arm. Can you imagine?'

'No.'

'Not the sort of thing a girl should see.'

'How old were you?'

'Six or seven.'

'That's young…'

'The older I get the clearer those days become. I can smell the food we ate, and hear the crowds. Soup kitchens. We used to eat at soup kitchens.'

'We had soup kitchens in the war.'

'Where?'

'London.'

'I like London,' she said. 'That's where you were born?'

'Yes.'

We reached the garden, and I went first, skirting the vegetables until I reached the shed in the corner. I said, 'Know how to use a rake?'

'I don't know what a rake is.'

'Here.' I pulled one out of the stack of tools. 'I'll show you.'

There were carrots to sow, the flavoursome variety called Short 'n' Sweet. I had a packet of seeds in my jacket pocket. I had dug the ground in the winter, spread manure, allowed frosts to break the clods, and had forked it over. Now I took the rake, and starting at the top of the garden, began to work my way down. I stopped halfway, held the small of my back and said, 'There's nothing to it.'

'Are you all right?'

'Yes…' I bent and picked up a stone. 'If you find any of these, sling them on the pile.'

'Have you got a pair of gloves?'

'They'll be big.'

She tucked her shirt in and hitched her trousers. 'I'm getting used to big.'

'Okay.' I shouldered the rake and went back to the shed. There was a pair of leather gloves on a shelf, next to a pile of dirt and a jam jar of rusted screws I had been meaning to soak in oil. 'They'll be massive.'

'Blisters or massive,' she said. 'I think I'll go with massive.' She put them on. They made her arms look like paddles. 'Pass me the thing.'

I passed it.

'Thanks.'

'What day is it?'

'Wednesday.'

She laughed. 'When I saw this place I thought I'd stumbled into a nightmare.' We were sitting to watch the sun set. 'What twenty-four hours can do.'

I nodded but said nothing. I had been thinking the same. I was reminded of Marianne, drinking in a small café on the waterfront with people strolling by, pigeons pecking around our feet.

'Twenty-four hours…'

I raised my glass.

She raised hers.

The air was scented with wood smoke, the sun whispered into the sea and the sky wrote music across its face. A split cloud split and that split split, and shreds sparked across the water.

'You think you could never get used to something, but how wrong can you be?'

'What are you talking about?'

'This place. The longer I'm here the more I like it. The more I need it.'

'That's how I feel.'

'You need it?'

'Yes.'

'Need,' she whispered. 'Want,' she said, and that word hung in the air. 'I want another twenty-four hours.' *Thank you for everything*. She sipped her drink, and took a deep breath. The cat came from the house and strolled across the yard to the ruined cottages. There was a wren nesting there, and she was going to have it. 'The quiet is a need, isn't it?'

I agreed.

'I love it so much.'

I mumbled, 'You're welcome.' It was all I could manage.

'Are you sure about that?'

'Yes.'

'Jacob's expecting me tomorrow.'

'Where?'

'London. We're flying back at the weekend.'

'I'll go to Zennack tomorrow. Give me his number and I'll give him a call.'

'You don't know what you're saying.' She stared into her drink. 'He's very persuasive. There's nothing he likes more than a challenge.'

'I've known men like that.'

'I don't know,' she said. 'Jacob's different to other people. No one's ever said no to him.'

'Maybe it's time someone did.'

'I should have spent more time with him.'

'Don't regret the past. It's a waste of time. There's nothing you can do about it.'

'That's easy to say.'

'Would you regret not having another day here?'

'Oh, yes. I want to go swimming again. And I want to see you sow some more carrots.'

'Then stay.'

'He won't like it…'

'I'd like it,' I said, and I reached over and put my hand on her arm. I shivered. She looked down at it.

'I bet you would.'

I took the hand away.

'Hey,' she said. 'It's okay.'

'I'm sorry.'

'Forget it,' she said, and her voice chimed with loss and fright. The air was squeezed between us. I poured myself another vodka, and she lit a cigarette.

'I can't do that,' I said, and I meant it. I meant it more than I had ever done.

You don't know how quickly I realised that I never wanted you to leave, how complete you made me feel. You, my house, the dog, the fireplace.

I thought I was past falling so deeply, tumbling like a boy in scuffed shoes and a torn jacket.

You never said something without thinking first, you were stronger than all the things you had done, you had a girlish way of looking away and twirling a lock of your hair.

You had beautiful ears, and I wanted to rub their lobes.

I was sixty-eight years old. You were seven when I was born. What were you doing when I was seven? When I was twenty? Forty?

Did you think I was a handsome man? If I'd written to you, would you have replied? It doesn't matter, not any more.

You said you wanted another twenty-four hours. You didn't add '… with you', but I added those words myself. I heard you say them in my mind and that was enough.

You said, 'Why can't you forget whatever it is?'

'You…' I said, and I tried to force my feelings out, but they would not come.

'Yes?' she said.

'Please,' I said. 'Stay as long as you want.'

'Do you know what you're saying?'

'I don't care…'

'You're very kind,' she said.

'You make me kind.'

'What? How can I do that? I don't know you.'

'Does that matter?'

'What are you talking about, Michael?'

I shook my head now, and ran my fingers through my hair. 'I don't know,' I said.

13

Captain Perkins of the SS *Mademoiselle Mabry* was a small and unusual man. He mixed easily with his crew, officers and men, and uniquely among captains I knew, never ate alone. He was clean-shaven and always wore his cap. I sailed with him for three years from 1961, mainly on Mediterranean and West African runs.

In 1958 his son had died while he was chartered in the Pacific, and he couldn't get home for two months. This tragedy, and his failure to be with his wife and child when it mattered, had scarred but not reduced him. He took solace in his crew; he treated them like a family. He recognised my grief and guilt, and though he was not a bitter man, told me that time did not heal. When I told him that I couldn't stop dreaming about my mother, he said that all I could do was punish myself. I had to drown the guilt. I told him that I had tried to. I hadn't been with a woman for over a year, I never went ashore, I lay on my bunk and read Russian novels. I drank alone.

'You call that a punishment?'

I didn't know what to say.

'You must do more.'

'How, sir?'

'That's up to you.'

'What did you do, sir?'

'That's for me to know.'

If his son had lived he would have been my age. Captain Perkins was frank with me, and explained that he wanted to imagine I was his son. I told him about my father and he shook his head. He asked to see my cap, and ran his fingers around the lining. 'Mate told me you were a lucky one,' he said.

'I don't feel it, sir.'

'Luck's got nothing to do with what you feel, or how. Luck makes its own rules.'

'I know, sir. My mother told me.'

'And you can't break them.' He gave me my cap back. 'Don't lose it.'

'I'm not going to, sir.'

We were carrying coal to Alexandria, ballasting to Odessa, loading Ukrainian grain and returning to the Tyne. The Black Sea was wild and unpredictable; we were stuck in Odessa for a week, sheltering from nines and tens.

I decided how I would punish myself. I threw a half-read book into the dock, watched it sink, went into town and did not buy a woman. I flirted with one but when the time came to leave the bar I shook my head and ordered another drink. She slapped my face and spat at my feet, and stormed into the night. I asked for the bottle, and beckoned another woman.

She came to my table. Her pimp watched from the back door. I asked him to join us. He was reluctant. I stood up and put up my fists, pushed the woman away and told him to fight. If my drink wasn't good enough for him then he could fight. I stepped up. He pulled a knife.

The bar cleared, a woman screamed, glasses broke. Money rolled across the floor. The barman picked up a phone and began to dial. I took another step forward, lunged and slipped. The pimp caught me as I fell, aimed for my chest and stabbed my arm.

The pain was not what you would expect. It came as a thud from a long way off, a dull sound you try to place but can't, and then suddenly it's on top of you, pushing in all directions. I looked down, saw blood, looked up, saw the blade again, shouted, the blade was grabbed, the pimp floored and the barman put the phone down.

Blood, beer and ambulance. I remember the ambulance but I don't remember the hospital. I was patched up, discharged and went to another bar.

I wanted to be hurt and humiliated in public. I wanted people to point and guess that I had abandoned my mother in London, in a damp flat where the dust settled on her head. Odessa was a dark city and matched my mood. I drank vodka, I slept alone in a room over a bar and listened to the windows rattle through the storms.

Do the dead think? Do they appreciate the livings' sacrifice to guilt? Do the dead know what guilt is? Dead man's hand, dead man's face, are you the one with dead man's eyes, wrapped in a piece of his dead wife's lace? When we sailed for the Tyne in February 1961, I had been hit by a dozen Odessan women, and threatened with guns. I forgot one Tuesday completely. I was covered in bruises, and walked with a limp. The passage was slow, and I had time to think. Next time I saw Steffi I would ask her to bind me to the frame she kept in her back bedroom, and I would not scream for mercy.

'I don't think my mother wanted to leave this place, but she didn't have any choice. She wanted to come back one day. When we left New York, when we started west, I think she imagined she wouldn't stop until she got home. America was never her home. She missed this.' Elizabeth pointed. 'But she died.'

'When?'

'Nineteen-forty.'

'What did you do?'

'We were living in Anaheim, California. She worked in the orange groves. I worked in the orange groves. The farmer's sister took me in. She had six kids. I suppose one more didn't make any difference. She'd promised Mother.'

We were sitting outside to eat supper. I had cooked some eggs and bacon, and sliced some bread. The food was spread out on a tea chest. I had lit a lamp and hung it from the porch.

A fishing boat appeared around the point, its lights blazing, engine chugging, steaming slowly north. Gulls fluoresced over its stern. Their cries drifted on the breeze to where we sat.

'The farmer sold out. They built Disneyland over the groves.' She shook her head. 'I went back down there a few years ago. I don't recognise Anaheim now.'

The boat turned and began to steam south, taking a course parallel to the first.

'The farmer made a fortune and moved downtown. Bought a plot of land and built a hotel. The Desmond. It's still there, but it's nothing like it used to be. It was a grand place.'

I watched her face as she talked. Her cheeks were full of blood and the creases around her eyes were like the crinkled petals of pink flowers. I wanted to touch them and then smell my fingers.

I don't think she had thought about the flattened orange groves of Anaheim for years. The years devour events, memory grows lazy, life forgets its reason. The ocean comes to the shore and fingers the rocks along the tideline. Motels grow where trees stood, and cars park where men sharpened scythes. Cows and sheep grazed where aeroplanes land, but the sky never changes.

'He was always there at the right place, at the right time. He was a lucky man.'

'Who?'

'Frank. The farmer, except you never said he used to be a farmer. He was a hotelier now, a good one too. He built a private cinema for his guests, and you could order anything off any menu at any time of day or night. Breakfast at one, dinner in the morning.' She dipped some bread in her egg. 'I don't think he ever served a supper like this.'

'Is it good?'

'Yes, Michael.' She tossed a piece of bacon to the dog, leant towards me and patted my arm. 'Good. Better and better.' She smiled. 'When did I last feel like this?'

'At the Desmond?'

'Maybe. Maybe, before I met Joe Leben.'

'The producer?'

'Yeah… How did you know that?'

I shrugged and tapped my head.

'Yeah…' She gave me a long look, then said, 'Joe Leben… He told Frank that I'd be perfect in a picture he was putting together. I think Frank was glad to see the back of me, but it was the only excuse I needed. I was out of there.' She looked sternly at me, and pointed a finger. 'Ambition's a killer, Michael, and I had it bad.'

'Not any more?'

'A little.'

'What was the film?'

'*Little Jennie*.'

'I didn't see that one…'

'You're lucky.'

'I saw most of them…'

'You were a fan?'

'More than that.' I looked at the floor and tapped my head again. I told her: 'I was nuts. Kept a scrapbook. Used to cut out your pictures, newspaper clippings, that sort of thing.'

'You didn't!'

'I almost wrote to you once. After *Missing You*.'

'I'm missing you already…' she breathed, exactly as she did in the film. Exactly. In my house. But then the face cracked, and she looked away with a grim look and thin, pursed lips, and she could have been someone else completely, some dangerous stranger with a hidden reason.

I first saw *Missing You* in 1946, in Liverpool, and I've seen it at least half a dozen times since. I can recall every scene.

The opening credits roll over an evening sky. The camera slowly pans from the zenith to the horizon. The clouds thin, and a Manhattan skyline appears.

As the credits fade, we pick up street sounds, reach ground level, move down the street and stop outside a hotel. Guests come and go. We focus on a couple who come from the hotel, descend the steps and walk slowly towards us. The man is George (Richard Wood) and the woman is Jane (Elizabeth Green). They stop and stand at the foot of the steps. She has medium-length blonde hair, and wears a pale coat. He wears a broad-rimmed hat and a dark coat. She shivers, and he holds her tight.

The camera closes on her face, and she says, 'I'm missing you already.'

'Me too, darling.'

'I love you so much.'

He is leaving for the Middle East, where he will be supervising the construction of a bridge. She is not going to see him for six months...

An aeroplane is waiting at the airport. Its exhaust fumes blow across the foggy runway, the propellers feather and a piano plays a single chord. The lovers kiss and then George breaks away. Jane is left standing, her hand raised...

The night becomes day, and the garden of a house in upstate New York. Jane is sitting in a deckchair, birds are singing, leaves are rustling. A woman (her mother) appears from the house, hesitates, then crosses the lawn. She is white-faced, and has been crying. She wipes her cheeks. 'Oh, Jane,' she says, and Jane turns, surprised.

The mother opens her mouth to speak, but the words stick in her throat. Jane says, 'What's the matter?'

'George...'

'Mother?'

'I think you'd better come indoors.'

'No! Tell me what's happened!'

'There's been an accident. George's plane. It had some sort of engine failure.'

Jane's eyes dim. 'Is he dead?'

'I don't know. Father's on the phone now.'

'I think…' says Jane, 'I think I will come indoors.' Need is in her eyes, and in her mouth…

The birds do not stop singing, but then their tunes change… they are harsh, the light is harsh and the camera is tracking a trail of smoking wreckage, shards of glass, ruptured suitcases. A teddy bear, a paperback book with singed pages. Another squawk, then only the sound of the wind and the gentle crackle of fires.

We are in the Middle East. Bare hillsides straddle the horizon.

Slowly, we become aware of the noise of stumbling feet. An electrical circuit in the plane's cockpit explodes. Sparks fly, illuminating the dead face of the pilot. The camera closes on the face of the man with the stumbling feet, and we recognise him as George. He is staring towards the sound of the explosion. The camera pulls back, and we see his ripped shirt, bruised face, and a bleeding wound on his forehead. His eyes are wide, staring. The camera continues to retreat, revealing more wreckage, smoke, carnage. George stares at the sun and slowly sinks to his knees. The camera is retreating faster now, until we can see the whole scene…

A bedroom, a single woman's room. A dressing table, folded clothes on a chair, a picture of horses galloping along a wind-swept beach hangs over a plain chest of drawers. The light is dim; the curtains waft in a gentle breeze. They are half closed.

Jane is lying in bed, staring at the moon through the gap in the curtains. Her mother sits beside her.

'Oh, Jane. Jane.'

Jane cannot speak. She holds a handkerchief to her face. Mother opens her mouth to say something more, then shakes her head. A single violin, a piano chord...

In the desert, George is walking, dragging his feet. He is concentrating, staring straight ahead. He is willing himself to carry on, to live. He climbs a dune, stops and looks down. He sinks to his knees but does not fall. He must keep going. He has a water bottle slung across his chest. He reaches for it, and takes a swig. The precious stuff dribbles down his chin and wets his shirt. He puts his hand up to catch the drips, and sucks his fingers.

Suddenly, his eye is caught by a distant light. This wasn't there last time he looked. It flickers in the evening gloom, but when he focuses on it, it disappears. For a moment he thinks the desert is playing tricks on him. He strains towards the place where the light was, and it reappears. It's joined by another. George stands and begins to stumble down the dune...

A thousand miles away, Jane and her mother are walking down a street. They stop at a park gate. We can see a duck pond, benches, a small café. 'I think,' says Jane, 'I'm going to sit down for a while.' She points to the café, and her mother nods.

The park... mothers with babies in prams, small children bending down to feed the ducks.

Elderly people sit on benches and cluck with contentment, and a policeman strolls by. Jane and Mother appear, and come to a foreground café table. Jane sits but Mother does not. Mother says, 'You'll be all right?'

'Yes, Mother. Don't fuss.'

Mother is going to have her hair done.

Jane buys a cup of coffee, sits back and drinks.

Inside the café, a man is sitting at a table, smoking a cigarette. He is looking at Jane, whose sad eyes are following the progress of a little girl who skips around the edge of the pond.

The man stubs his cigarette out, stands, drops some coins on the table and goes to the door.

He walks to Jane's table. She is smiling at the little girl, and he says, 'I was beginning to think you'd forgotten how to smile.'

'Bob?'

'Hello, Jane...'

And we're in a Bedouin camp. A group of men are sitting on the ground around a fire. They drink coffee and talk in whispers. Their tents are ranged around, and camels are tethered beyond. The fire and a pair of burning tapers cast a warm but sinister light.

A camel grunts, then another, and one of the men turns to look. Something catches his eye. He speaks to his neighbour, and the two men stand, gather their robes and walk into the gloom.

They walk to the edge of the camp, until the firelight cannot penetrate the night. They peer into it. One shrugs and the other mumbles under his breath. They are about to turn away when suddenly, frighteningly, George stumbles out of the gloom and collapses in the sand at their feet. Immediately the men shout for their companions, who come running. George is turned over. His face is burnt and scabby, and his clothes hang in tatters. His shoes are missing. Four men pick him up and carry him across the camp to a tent.

The tent is lit by oil lamps. Rugs cover the floor; a raised bed is set at one end. George is laid down. One man brings a bowl of water and a cloth, sits beside him and gently dabs at his face. George opens his eyes. They are dim. He tries to focus, but cannot...

Bob stands on a New York street. He wears a hat and coat, and carries a newspaper. He crosses the road and enters a café. Jane is sitting at a window table. He takes off his hat, smooths his hair, sits opposite her and says, 'How are you today?'

She shakes her head. 'I don't know.'

A waitress comes to the table and says to Bob, 'What would you like?'

'Jane?'

'I'm fine.'

'Coffee,' says Bob. 'Black.'

The waitress leaves the table and goes to the counter.

Jane says, 'They found the wreckage.'

'I know.' He puts the newspaper on the table.

'No survivors.'

Bob reaches across the table and takes Jane's hand. She makes no move to avoid his touch…

A string of camels is moving slowly across a barren plain. The sun is low; dust rises. One of the camels is rigged with a canopy. Beneath this, swaying with the motion, George lies, propped by cushions. He is tired but recovering. He has been fed, and his wounds are patched.

At a cry from the head of the caravan, the camels stop and a boy offers water to the men. He comes to George, and passes a ladle. George manages a smile, the boy beams back, another cry and the caravan moves off again…

Bob and Jane are sitting on a hillside. The remains of a picnic are scattered around. Jane closes her eyes, leans back to catch the sun on her face. Bob wants to say something. He leans towards her and says, 'Jane?'

'Yes?'

He shakes his head. He can't say what he wants. He gestures at the wreckage of the meal, turns away and mumbles, 'We should have brought another bottle.'

'I'm sorry?' Jane opens her eyes now, and looks at him. He looks so sad. She reaches out and touches his shoulder; as she does, he turns suddenly, and kisses her on the mouth.

The shock is total, for both of them. She pulls away; he jumps up and takes a step back. 'Oh God,' he says. 'I'm sorry…'

An oasis. The caravan approaches, the camels stop and kneel. Palm trees sway over whitewashed houses. Goats browse, children play.

The caravan master calls for assistance, and George is helped down and carried to a house. 'No,' he says, and he insists on walking.

As he is carried, an unshaven European (Alex) watches from a distance. Dressed in a scruffy white linen suit, he scratches his armpits. He looks towards the house where George is taken, but does not move...

Jane is driving. She is alone, and doesn't know where she's going. She drives fast, her face streaked with tears. Confusion is her companion.

She approaches a deserted crossroads. She doesn't notice a red light. She wipes her nose. A truck is approaching. Its driver gives a long hoot on his horn. Jane doesn't hear. Another hoot, and another. Jane jumps the red light, the truck swerves. She swerves, hits the verge and stops. The truck slews to a halt. Dust settles.

Jane sits and stares at the night. The truck driver climbs down from his cab and runs across the road. He reaches the car. He's angry. He yells, 'What the hell are you doing?' He sees Jane. Tears are pouring from her eyes. She turns her face to look at him. Her features appear to be melting, dripping away.

'Hey, lady,' says the driver. 'Are you okay?'

Jane says nothing.

'Lady?'

Nothing.

The engine ticks over. The wind whines. The driver taps the roof of Jane's car, shakes his head and returns to his truck. He climbs into the cab, the air brakes blow, he drives away. Jane doesn't move...

George and Alex sit on a low wall, beneath swaying palms. George says, 'So the nearest telephone's fifty miles?'

'Correct,' says Alex. 'You can be there in a couple of days.'

'A couple of days? It's only fifty miles.'

'It's rough country. You should know that.'

George nods and says, 'But I've got to try.' He knows Alex is telling the truth. He was once a respected archaeologist; a doomed love affair with a local girl brought him to this place; a broken heart and palm wine have kept him here.

'The caravan doesn't leave for a week.'

'A week?'

'If you're lucky.'

'Then I'll rent a camel.'

Alex laughs. 'Do you know what you're saying?'

'And you can show me the way. You do know the way, don't you?'

'Me?'

'You've got to help, Alex.' George's face pleads.

'I'm not the man I was.'

'Please, Alex.'

The Englishman cannot say no. He can glimpse the possibility of redemption, one last chance. He scuffs his shoes in the dirt, rubs the sweat from his palms then turns to George and nods slowly...

Jane's car, parked as we saw it before. She stares through the windscreen, then sits up, turns the key in the ignition and reverses into the road. She drives away from us, into a grey and threatening morning...

George is in the desert again, this time with purpose. He leads a camel. Alex trudges behind. The camel is loaded with bedrolls, a tent, food and water. The two men say nothing...

Bob is sitting in an empty bar, nursing a whisky at the counter. The barman, a fat and weary man, moves towards him and says, 'It's like this. You move on.'

'Hey, Frank. Give me a break.'

Frank takes a glass and pours himself a soda. 'Regret for the past is a waste of the spirit.'

'Are you telling or selling?'

'Just trying to help, Bob. You did wrong. You know it. Life's a bastard.'

'It's more than that, Frank.' He finishes his drink and pushes his glass forward.

Frank takes down a bottle and pours another shot. 'How much more?'

Bob shakes his head. 'All the way. Problem is, I bought a one-way ticket. I can't get back.'

'To what?'

'I dream about her, Frank. I never did that before. Not with any woman…'

We are on a bluff overlooking a deep canyon in upstate New York. The moon is full, the silence is deep. Car headlights swing across the scene, disappear and reappear moments later, close now, and bright. The car stops, the lights go out, the door opens and Jane climbs out. She walks to the edge of the bluff, and stops. She stares down. Confusion and guilt mark her face, and the wind blows her hair. A hooting owl crosses the canyon. Its call alarms Jane, who turns to watch its flight.

She takes a packet of cigarettes from her pocket, and lights one. The owl calls again, distant now. She holds the lighter up, so we can read the words 'To my darling' engraved on its side. She lights it again then throws it at the sky. We watch it fall, still alight, tumbling and flaming into the darkness below. It clatters against the rocks, it goes out…

In the desert, the night comes down, and a chill wind with it. Stars speckle the sky. George, Alex and the camel trudge on. They reach the top of a dune, and stop. George sniffs the air and says, 'I can smell it.'

'What?' Alex is irritated, tired and thirsty. He takes a water bottle from his pack, and drinks carefully. He wipes his mouth with the back of his hand.

'The sea.' George drops the camel's halter and walks forward. 'Yes,' he says. Alex comes to him and puts a hand on his shoulder. 'Thank you, Alex.'

Alex smiles. We haven't seen him smile much. He needed that drink of water. He says, 'I didn't do this for your sake, old man.'

'I know you didn't.' George is a perceptive man. He scratches his ear and says, 'How far is it?'

'One more day.'

George takes another deep breath and says again, 'The sea.' His face is bright, as if illuminated from within. Alex reflects this illumination, shining with the redemption he has been seeking...

Jane, returned from her flight to the canyon, is sitting at a café table, talking with her mother. The older woman is not wearing a hat. She says, 'I understand,' and stirs a cup of coffee.

'I don't believe George is dead. I've got this feeling he's alive. I want him to be so much. So much...'

'I know.'

'But Bob... Bob has made me think again.'

'That's a perfectly understandable reaction. No one's blaming you.'

'I feel so guilty.'

'Of course you do.'

'It's awful, but I can't help myself.'

'Honestly, Jane...'

'I think about George, about the things we used to do, the places we used to go, but then Bob gets in the way, and I'm wondering if he would like to see some of those places, do some of those things.'

Mother leans across the table and takes Jane's hand. 'It's going to be all right, darling.'

Jane looks up with disbelief in her eyes. 'Is it?' she says.

'Yes...'

George and Alex have reached a busy coastal town. They have recovered from their walk, found somewhere to stay, eaten a meal, and now Alex is taking George to a telegraph office.

They walk through the thronging streets, past hawkers and beggars, hustlers and priests. Boys play tag, a donkey stands with its head bowed. George stops at a shop and buys something sticky to eat.

Alex is washed and shaved, and wearing a fresh shirt. He walks with a new purpose. They reach the office…

Jane and Bob are sitting in a quiet restaurant. Their main course has just arrived. As Bob examines his food, she says, 'I'm as much to blame as you are.'

'I don't like that word. It implies guilt, and I don't think either of us is guilty. If George was here, he wouldn't accuse us of anything.'

Jane looks at a potato. 'I've got to know what happened to him.' She cuts it.

'Of course…'

'But you know what I feel about you.'

'No, I don't.'

'I like you, Bob. I really do. And you've been so good to me.'

'The other day…'

'Forget it.'

'I can't.'

Jane blushes. 'Nor can I. But we can't go on like that. Not until I know.'

'No.'

She runs a finger around the rim of her glass, picks it up and drinks. 'I must tell you…'

'What?'

The drink fortifies her. 'I'm going to Egypt.'

'Egypt?'

'Yes.'

'What do you expect to find there?'

She shrugs. 'I don't know. Probably nothing. But I can't just sit here, wondering.'

So much is unspoken. The scene is charged with unasked questions, hesitant answers. Bob says, 'I'll miss you.' Jane drinks some wine. Bob waits; when she says nothing, he returns to his food. She looks at him, then focuses on a couple on the far side of the restaurant. They have finished their meal, and are flirting over coffee and liqueurs. Bob looks up, then follows her eyes to them. He turns back, clears his throat and offers more wine. She puts her hand over her glass and says, 'I'm fine...'

George has left the desert port, bound for Marseille. He stands on deck and the salt air bathes his face. The sun is setting in tumbling showers of orange and red. The sea burns. He is joined at the rail by the mate, a burly man who wears a skewed cap and says, 'It doesn't matter how many times I see one, they still stop me in my tracks.'

George nods.

'God had a good day.'

George agrees.

Voices shout, and something clatters on deck. The mate ignores the noise. He is transfixed. The shore has disappeared; the sea is immense. It rolls slowly, as if sluggish beasts are moving beneath its surface. A bird passes overhead, and shit drops on George's hat. He takes it off, smiles and says. 'That's lucky, isn't it?'

The mate turns and says, 'I don't believe in luck.'

George turns to face the man, and asks, 'What do you believe in?'

'Work. I like work. Luck I hate. I saw men who died for luck.'

'Did you?'

The mate says, 'I did,' but doesn't elaborate. George turns away, nodding to himself, thinking maybe the mate's right.

The sunset fades, and we fade with it. A familiar chord is heard, and another, and the plaintive melody of 'Missing You'...

Jane's mother is screaming down a hall, waving a telegram. 'He's alive!' she yells, taking the stairs at a trot, rushing along the landing and into her daughter's bedroom. 'He's alive!' Jane sits up. 'George?' she says.

'Yes.'

The two women embrace...

A thronging Marseille street. Bars, dockers, land-happy sailors. A man plays a trumpet on the pavement, and a woman sidles up to him. People stop to listen. Before he reaches the second verse, Jane and her mother appear. They are looking for a café.

They leave the main street and enter a narrow alley. The trumpet fades. A woman stares from a ground-floor window, and ignores them as they pass. A cat crosses their path. They turn a corner and stop. They look at the street name. Mother nods, and they walk on.

Another cat, and then a pool of light from a café window. The trumpet fades to a whisper. They approach the window, and stop. The world seems to stop. Jane's mother releases her arm and peers inside. She nods again. Jane turns and says a word, hesitates, puts her hand on the door knob. Mother smiles. Jane enters the café.

The café is quiet. Check cloths on round tables, bentwood chairs, a polished counter. A cheerful owner with a cloth over his shoulder and his sleeves rolled up. A pair of lovers at a corner table, other tables in shadow.

Jane closes the door, takes a step forward, stops. The owner's eyes swivel from Jane towards one of the shadowed tables. A hand appears from the shadow, and rests on the table. A chair scrapes.

'Jane?'

'George?'

The chair is pushed back and George stands. He comes from the shadow. His face is clean-shaven. Jane rushes forward. They fall into each other's arms. The owner turns and reaches up for a bottle.

'Darling.'

Jane's voice breaks to a whisper. 'Missing you was torture. Every minute was an hour...'

'I know...'

'... every day was a year.' They loosen their embrace, and look into each other's eyes. Jane says, 'How long has it been?'

'Too long, my darling.'

We close on Jane's face again and it burns from the screen. The flawless face shining with tears, and the voice that comes from miles away. 'I love you so much.' Her shivering lips. This is how millions remember Elizabeth Green, and why. The relief and joy in her eyes are touched with doubt. For a moment she thinks about Bob, and we do, but then George embraces her again, and they kiss.

We are drifting away from the scene, away from the café, and we can hear the trumpet again. Strings join in, and a piano, and then we are on the street, leaving the lovers to themselves.

'I saw it half a dozen times. I know it off by heart.'

'You had me bad?'

'I thought I could make you happy.'

'Did you?' She laughed, but it wasn't funny.

'Yes.'

She finished her food, wiped her fingers, went for her cigarettes, pulled one out, lit up, blew smoke and said, 'You thought you could make me happy?'

I nodded.

'How the hell could you have made me happy?' She gave her voice an edge. 'What did you know about me?'

I swallowed. 'I was young. Sometimes I didn't see a woman for months at a time...'

'So you'd have been a lot of use.' She jabbed a finger, crossed her legs and glared at me.

'Please,' I said. I wished the earth would open up. 'I didn't mean to...'

'No, you didn't, did you? You didn't think.'

'You're wrong. I thought too much. Sometimes it was all I did.'

'You thought you could be the man I needed, but an idea like that's got nothing to do with thinking.' She banged the table with the palm of her hand. 'Nothing at all.'

'I didn't say anything about need.'

'Isn't that all there is?'

'I was talking about being happy.'

'What's happiness got to do with it?' She was shouting now. Her breath stank.

'Don't give yourself a heart attack.'

'And I suppose you know all about them.'

'Enough. I've seen a few.'

'Caused a few too?'

'Forget it.' This was as angry as I wanted to hear her, and she was building for more.

'You think I should?'

'Yes,' I said. 'Please.' I pleaded.

She looked away and uncrossed her legs. She took a long drag at her cigarette, blew the smoke at the ceiling and held up a hand. 'I will,' she said. 'No problem.'

A heart attack finished Captain Perkins. He was standing on the starboard bridge wing, watching the Liberian coast. The sun was setting beyond the trees. No lights shone on land. The place looked deadly. A week before, I had paid a woman to stub out her cigarette in the palm of my hand. He turned to me and said, 'My son wanted me to bring him to Africa.' A moment later he gripped his chest and lurched forward. I grabbed him, he slipped to the deck and I yelled for help. His cap fell off and I was shocked to discover that he was bald. 'Don't punish yourself for ever,' he said. His eyes rolled and he suffered a massive spasm. I tried to hold him as he died but he flailed and cried out and I could not get close to him. I tried to break through the barrier of rank but that was impossible. I wanted to take his hand and let him know that I was there. I wanted to tell him that he had been some sort of father to me for three years but he died, I had no chance. Help came and stood over us but I didn't know who. I was taken to one side while the body was carried away. I went below to drink a beer but I didn't cry for him. A sailor must be a man. We buried him off the Liberian coast, over the Romanche Fracture.

A sailor must be a man and take his punishment, but not for ever. As Captain Perkins's corpse flipped into the sea I felt pointless. I was thirty-five. I had nothing to show for anything. I was going nowhere. One day I could be captain but then I would be buried at sea, no one to weep for me, no home. A hole in the ocean where my body used to be, a line of men standing at the railing, nothing. I didn't want to see the world like this any more.

The night came slowly, creeping over the ruins and my house. I lit the fire. She drank and said, 'I wasn't shouting at you. I'm angry with myself. You're just the one I'm taking it out on. What you said about your scrapbook, cutting my picture out. That was sweet.' We were sitting next to each other. She reached out and took my hand, and ran her fingers over it.

'Is it your son?'

'Hell, no,' she said. 'He's just an asshole. No. It's more than that.'

'Are you going to tell me?'

'Don't push it,' she said, and she patted the back of my hand.

'Tell me. Please.'

'Please?'

I reached for the vodka, poured and said, 'If it helps.'

She took a long drink, tipped her head back and let her hair fall over the back of the couch. 'How long have I been here?'

'A couple of days.'

'A couple of days,' she said. 'That's all it ever took.'

'What?'

'That first walk, when you went to fetch the cab. When I was thinking that this place was great because of what it didn't have — phones, cars, you know — and now I'm thinking it's great because of what it does have.' She let go of my hand. 'You've got all you need, haven't you?'

'I think so,' I said.

She looked around the kitchen. 'Everything. This isn't a nightmare at all.'

'It's a good dream,' I said.

'I can see that.'

The fire crackled, the door rattled, the cat turned over, the dog dreamt. I decided what to say, ran the words through my head once, twice, again. I rubbed my eyes and took a deep breath. I tasted vodka and then I blurted, 'You can stay as long as you want.'

Immediately: 'No I can't.'

'Why not?'

She sat up, lit a cigarette and said, 'Why do you think?'

'I don't know,' I said.

'Forget it.'

'Why?'

'Michael!' she snapped, then turned away. I reached out, took her chin in my hand and turned her back. 'Don't!' She hit my hand away; I backed off. She looked at her cigarette, threw it away, drank some vodka and said, 'Don't!' again.

I remembered how I used to talk to a slack crew. I deepened my voice. 'Tell me why you can't stay.'

100

'Please…' She slumped and rubbed her forehead. 'This time last week I was sitting on the porch at home having a manicure. Bob Mitchum called, we had a few drinks, talked about the old days…' She looked down at her trousers, my trousers, and took a deep breath. 'I was wearing Versace.'

'What's Versace?' I said.

She looked at me, and the colour of her face changed from grey to pink in seconds, her lips trembled and she laughed. She leant towards me, patted my knee and did not stop.

'What did I say?'

She laughed louder.

'Elizabeth?'

'Please…' She looked away and stopped, looked at me again and started again. I reached out and took her hand, and she clasped it, rubbed it and mumbled, 'I never met one like you.'

'No.'

'I should have.'

What could I say? I wanted to kiss her. I tried, 'This is like a movie.'

'No it's not,' she said. 'This is nothing like a movie. This is more like being *at* the movies. Waiting for the next move.'

'And what's that?'

'You tell me.'

I gave her a serious look. 'I think Dunn's got a special offer on shower units.'

'What?'

'And I'm going to finish the bedroom. I've been putting it off.'

'Have you?'

'Yes,' I said. 'All I need to do is get busy.'

'Busy's good.'

'Elizabeth?'

'Yeah?'

'If it makes any difference; if it does, I want you to stay…'

'Michael…'

'Listen!' I raised my voice. She shut up. 'When I came here I thought that this was it. I was happy. The house, the garden. The dog. But I suppose you don't know how happy you are until you see how happy you could be.'

'I'm not the person you think I am.'

'I'm not stupid,' I said. 'I know you're not straight out of *Missing You*. I don't know who you are.'

'Then why do you want me to stay?'

'I want to find out.'

'Sure,' she said.

'Think about it.'

'I already have.'

'And?'

She looked away from me but said nothing. Another cigarette, another log on the fire. I listened to her breathing, poured another drink and sat back to watch the lamps flicker. The kettle hissed on the back plate, the window plastic cracked. 'And?' I said again.

'I can't stay.'

14

I drove to Zennack in the morning. Daylight damages everything you think, it exposes one thought's holes, another's meaning. No meaning at all probably. As I was parking in the square, Mrs Bell came running with a message and a glint in her eye. 'Her son rang,' she puffed. 'Come on. I'll tell you.' She led me to her house and sat me in the kitchen.

'Elizabeth Green's son?'

'Yes. And he was quite charming.' She poured two cups of tea. 'He explained that his mother had a habit of... I can't remember the exact expression, but freaking something. Like she becomes a freak?'

I shrugged.

'And he was most apologetic. I was half expecting him to blame me.'

'Why would he do that?'

'I don't know. It was just a thought I had.'

'What else did he say?'

'Not much,' and now Mrs Bell's eyes widened and she gave me a huge smile. 'Except that he's coming down to fetch her.'

'What?' I felt my knees go.

'Yes.'

'When?'

Mrs Bell looked at her kitchen clock. 'This afternoon.'

'Today?'

'Yes,' she said, and my feet froze. 'His name's Jacob.'

'I know. Elizabeth told me about him.'

'What did she say?'

'Enough,' I said, and a silence settled between us. I looked out of the window and I knew that Mrs Bell's eyes were on me. Her dog sat up and scratched. I watched Mr Dunn come from his yard and cross the square to the pub. He went inside and came out a minute later with a drink. He sat on one of the pavement benches, lit a cigarette, sipped and waved to a passing car.

'I was thinking about what you said,' said Mrs Bell. 'About the cinema...'

'Yes?'

'Maybe we could go...'

'I thought you didn't think it would be a good idea.'

'I'm sorry.' She fidgeted with her collar. 'It's such a long time since I went out, and since my husband died I haven't thought about that sort of thing. It was very kind of you to ask, and I shouldn't have turned you down like that.'

'Please...'

She put her hands on the table, took a deep breath and said, 'I'd like to go to the cinema with you. We can take my car. I looked in the newspaper. You know what they're showing?'

'No.'

'*Raintown*.' She waited for my reaction. I gave nothing away. 'She's in it.'

'I know.'

'I would like to go. If your offer is still open…'

Mrs Bell was a very proper woman. In another life I could not have married her. We would not be growing old together. We would not be watching birds come to crusts on the lawn, or wondering about the weather. I did not want to ask her if she had a photograph of herself when she was twenty-one. I couldn't imagine her moist. I said, 'Of course it is. How about Saturday?'

'This Saturday?'

'Yes.'

She looked at me and I saw her thoughts in her face. Maybe she wanted to hold a man's arm on a crowded street and enjoy a drink in a bar. She said, 'I don't know what it'll be like.'

'What?'

'*Raintown*.' She lowered her voice. 'It does sound quite romantic.'

'I'm sure we'll enjoy it,' I said, and the phone rang.

Mrs Bell went to answer it, but while she talked I didn't think about going to the cinema. I didn't remember how moist one woman was, and how another was dripping. I wanted to go home. I wanted to tell Elizabeth Green that her son was on his way but that I would stand up for her. I would say no to him and warn him off my property. She could stay at Port Juliet as long as she liked. I could plaster the bedroom and plumb in one of Mr Dunn's special-offer shower units. I got up, and as I passed Mrs Bell in the hall, I whispered 'Goodbye' to her, and she put her hand over the mouthpiece and said, 'I'm sorry. It's a booking.'

'I've got to go. Thanks for the tea.'

'You're welcome,' she said, flustering and twirling the telephone cord.

'Saturday. I'll call for you.'

'Oh.' She almost dropped the phone. 'Yes. If you're sure...'

'Saturday,' I repeated, and I let myself out and crossed the square to the post office where I asked Mr Boundy for sixty cigarettes.

'Still with you, then, is she?' he said.

'I don't know,' I said.

Boundy twitched his moustache and his right eye closed slightly. Mrs Boundy dropped something in the back room. He didn't flinch. He put the cigarettes on the counter. 'She must smoke like a chimney.'

'Must she?' I said, and I showed him my teeth. He backed off. 'How much?'

'Six ninety-six.'

I put the money down, collected my change and left the shop.

My tractor does about twenty miles an hour. I drove in fourth all the way, startling sheep in their fields and a man on his bicycle. As I slewed down the road to Port Juliet I saw Elizabeth sitting on the beach, and she waved when she saw me. Her hair was down and she had tied her scarf around her neck. I parked badly and went to meet her. 'Your son's coming to fetch you.'

'When?'

'This afternoon.'

She looked at her watch. 'You're kidding.'

I shook my head.

She stood up, walked towards me, stopped, walked back and turned to look at the sea. 'How do you know?'

'He phoned Mrs Bell.'

'Mrs Bell?'

'At the guest house. You stayed there...'

'Sure,' she said. 'I remember.'

'So I didn't order the cab.'

'Okay... This afternoon?'

'Yes.'

She came to me now and said, 'Let's walk.'

We took the path away from the ruins, and as we climbed towards the point she took my arm. The sky was clear. She smoked. The wind was fresh and I felt anxious. I hadn't felt anxious for years. I looked at my hands, and they were shaking. The touch of her fingers and everything; I took deep breaths and breathed the clouds of her cigarette smoke. The sea wound itself up below us. The sun was high, our shadows short, and the grass waved all around us. A rabbit crossed our path, and an old ewe watched us pass. 'This *is* like a movie,' she said.

'*Dangerous Brew*,' I said. 'That was the first of yours I saw. I wanted to watch it for ever. I remember, it was like this. Like I want to see the world like this for ever.'

'Yeah,' she mumbled. 'Exactly. Exactly what I thought. Exactly like Baja.'

'What happened there?'

We reached the end of the path, and sat down on the slabs of rock that slope down to the point. 'After the film wrapped I drove south, ended up staying in a hotel on the coast. Hotel... I'm not sure that's the right word...' and she stopped for a moment to watch a flight of gulls swoop towards the offshore stacks. 'It looked derelict but the bar was stocked, and there were sheets on the bed. It was owned by an old army guy. Bob. He was like you.'

'How?'

'Big. Quiet.' She looked at me and blew smoke. 'Knew what he wanted to do. I booked in. The phone didn't work, the water didn't run but after a day I didn't care, after two days I was loving it, after three I wanted to stay. Then I got scared.'

'Why?'

106

'Because I wanted to stay.'

'Did you?'

'No.'

'Why not?'

'You know why not.'

'Okay.'

'But I always regretted that decision. I was never very brave. I still wonder what would've happened. It's what my mother did when she left this place. She cut all her ties. I wanted to do that but I couldn't.' She finished her cigarette and flicked the butt into the wind. 'It's still something I want to do.' She looked back towards the ruins. 'I want to learn how to grow vegetables.'

'I've got the book you'll need.'

She laughed and took my arm again. 'That's what I like about you, Michael. You're practical…'

'I have to be.'

'But that doesn't stop you thinking. It's a rare combination. Bob had it. He made me think.'

'Think as long as you want,' I said, and I laid my hand on hers. 'Stay as long as you want.'

'Staying's not as easy as thinking.'

'Then don't think about it.'

'You've lost me.'

I said, 'You could find yourself here.'

'Now you sound like a Californian.'

'Thanks.'

'You're welcome.'

'And so are you,' I said, meaning it, but the words were taken by the wind. Maybe she heard them, maybe she ignored them; whatever. She lit another cigarette and tipped her head back, and while I prayed so hard my lips moved, she closed her eyes to the day.

15

I was in the garden when I heard the cars. Dan came first. Jacob followed in a blue Mercedes. He drove with one hand on the wheel and his head sticking out of the window, edging around the potholes, slowly on to the verge and back again. Dan rolled along in neutral.

Elizabeth walked up from the house, laughed and said, 'You wouldn't think an asshole could drive a stick shift, would you?' I put my hoe down, and wiped my hands on my trousers.

Dan stopped behind the ruined terrace, climbed out of his car and rested against the bonnet. He lit a cigarette, took a deep drag and shook his head with meaning.

Jacob parked behind him, removed his sunglasses and sat for a moment, staring straight ahead. He did not look well. Elizabeth and I strolled down from the garden together, past the house, across the yard. The chickens scratched, the cat woke up, yawned and went back to sleep.

Jacob stepped out of his car, smoothed his trousers and said, 'Mother…'

'Jacob!'

'What are you doing?'

'Hello…'

'And what the hell are you wearing?'

'… Jacob.'

'Yeah?' he said.

'How are you?' she said, and she kissed his cheeks.

'Bushed.'

'I'm sorry…'

He put his hands on his hips, looked around and sighed. 'This is Baja again, isn't it?'

'No, Jacob, it isn't,' and 'This is Michael,' she said, and I put out my hand.

Jacob stared at it. 'Michael. Michael or Bob?'

'Michael,' I said.

'Sure,' he said. 'It's just you freeloaders all look the same to me.'

Jacob had fat hands, thick black hair and a wet moustache. His eyes were loaded with disappointment, his lips were moist, he had spent too long in the sun. His nose was full of blood. I reached out, took his hand and shook it before he had the chance to back off. I said, 'Welcome to Port Juliet.'

'You don't want to welcome me anywhere,' he said.

'Whatever...' I said.

'Try and be nice,' said Elizabeth.

He grunted.

Dan coughed, tossed his cigarette away and shuffled towards us. He was wearing the same clothes and the same expression he always wore; half removed from what was going on, brooding on a longing or a misplaced word. A girl he wanted back, a letter he wanted to write? The job he hated? He said, 'Are you going to need me any more?'

'I don't think so.' Jacob took out his wallet. 'What do I owe you?'

'Fifteen fifty.'

'What?'

'Fifteen fifty.' Dan didn't blink. His eyelids drooped, and he stood with his hands in his jacket pockets, his right knee thrust slightly forward.

'You're kidding! Christ!' Jacob didn't open the wallet. 'What for?'

'The taxi.'

'Pay the man,' said Elizabeth.

'But what's he done? Shown me the way from whatever that other place was and, what was it, five miles? Twenty bucks? Forget it!'

Elizabeth took out her own purse, gave Dan the money and said, 'Thanks...' Dan looked at her with a blank, almost dead expression.

Jacob said, 'What a rip-off.'

Dan turned and faced him, and for a moment I thought he was going to explode. His arms tensed, and his eyes widened, but then he turned, waved his hand over his head and without a word climbed into his car and drove away.

I offered to make tea and put some sugared biscuits on a plate but Jacob said 'I'm not staying' to me and 'Get your things' to Elizabeth.

'Why?' she said.

'You're coming with me.'

'When?'

'Now.'

'I don't think so.'

I think he laughed, but it was hard to tell. He made a chuckling sound and curled his lips, and displayed his teeth, but his eyes didn't crease or show any sparkle. 'Okay,' he said, 'what is it this time?'

'What do you mean?'

He looked at me and I knew that I would hit him. I tried to stop myself but I could not. I got the old tension in my head, and an increasing heat. My hands made fists and I rooted my feet. He was about four feet away, standing to my right. Elizabeth was to my left. His nose shone. He said, 'What's he got on you?' as if I wasn't there.

'Who?'

'Your latest friend.' He said 'latest' slowly, rolling the word around his mouth like a nut. He spat it out.

'Michael?' she said, and she moved to me and took my arm. 'You've got nothing on me, have you?'

I shook my head.

'But I think you've shown me something,' she said, 'that I'd forgotten.'

Jacob shifted on his feet, his eyes bulged a bit and he said, 'Like what, for God's sake?'

'Like this!' She looked around.

'You mean like Malibu except there're no houses, no people, no weather. Nothing.'

'You can't see?'

'What?'

'How can I explain?'

'Try, Mother.'

A lark began to sing, and another, and eight more tumbling through the sky. Their songs oiled the air, and combed it. 'The sun's shining...'

'Hey!' He leered. He had very regular teeth and thin lips, like the edges of a fresh cut. 'The sun only shines in California. Everywhere else it just glows a bit.'

'You don't believe that.'

'Try me.'

I'll try you. You have a mother and she loves you and you come down my road to my house and raise your voice with your Mercedes parked badly in front of the ruin of the house where your grandmother was born and you don't even ask about her. You don't wonder that she froze in that cottage through winters you couldn't imagine. You don't look at me. You don't think. You've done nothing, gone nowhere, seen nothing and my vision was going, slipping, gone. Head. Feet. I said nothing.

She said, 'Look at this place,' and she spread her arms.

'I'm looking.'

'It was where your grandmother was born, Jacob. Mary Green.' She pointed to the terrace. 'She lived in one of those cottages...'

'And had the sense to leave.'

'And always regretted it. She always planned a return.'

'Really? So what? You're doing it for her?'

Elizabeth nodded. 'You could say that. For her... and me.'

'You?'

'No one can touch me here.'

'Baja...' he hissed.

'I'm free. I can do what I want, and nobody has to know.'

'Like do what?'

'Dig the garden, mend a fence, feed the chickens...'

'Mend a fence? You want to mend a fence?'

'Sure. Why not?'

'You never mended a fence in your life.'

'So I'll start.'

'Okay,' he said, and with a deep breath, 'but at home. You can have all the freedom you want.' Another deep one. 'If we've been down on you that's our fault. Yeah. We'll make some changes.'

'You haven't been down on me. And there aren't any fences at home.'

'We could buy some.'

She laughed. 'No, Jacob, we couldn't. You can't buy fences like the ones here. They're special.'

'And he's special, is he?'

'You don't meet people like Michael in Malibu.'

'No,' he said 'You have to go to South Central.'

'You're not going to listen, are you?'

'I'll listen, but I won't believe you. I don't believe you believe yourself. How long's it taken you to get back to where you are now? Thirty years? Thirty years of wondering whether you can pay the rent, buy the groceries, and now you're going to blow it. How long have you waited for this?'

'What are you worried about, Jacob? Me blowing it or you not getting your slice?'

'We're not talking about me.'

'You just don't get it, do you? Your grandmother, my life. My needs. You know I have needs...'

He turned towards me, grinned and said, 'Selfish, isn't she?'

'No,' I said.

'It speaks.'

I hit him. I leapt on that man and started to pound him with his moustache and his very well-pressed trousers and his blue shirt buttoned to his throat. White socks. Beige slip-on shoes with gilt detail and we're on the ground and I'm punching his chest so he's blowing breath like this is it, I'm going to die, I won't see another morning, I'll never drink again, this man is killing me at the edge of a country I can't spell.

I'm breaking sweat. I can see my fists going slowly like I'm in a film and someone's going to tell me that's it, stop, don't do it any more, you've made your point. I can hear myself telling him to show some respect, be polite, wake up, but I know I've made a mistake, I shouldn't be doing this. But it's Odessa again and he's me, and I'm giving him the beating he deserves, the one he must take because he treats his mother like shit, he only wants her for what she can give him, he would forget her tomorrow if he could. He needs this. Elizabeth grabbed my shirt and pulled me back.

She had no strength in her arms but she could shout like you would not believe, right in my ear as I'm taking a chunk out of the man's shoulder with my teeth. He tastes sweet. 'Michael! No!' I turned to look at her and he scratched my cheek. 'Leave him!' I put my hand over his face and pushed him away. His head hit the ground, he let out a gasp of air, went limp and stopped struggling. I slapped him once more, stood up, straightened, took a handkerchief from my pocket and held it to my face. I turned to Elizabeth, wiped my brow and said, 'It can't fight.'

He wheezed, 'You're finished.'

'I haven't started…'

He pushed himself up. 'You're a maniac.'

'If I need to be.' I looked at Elizabeth and she was shaking, looking at her son, then at me, then back at him. She went for a cigarette.

He brushed his trousers and fingered his shoulder. He took a step, winced and said to her, 'You know how to pick them.'

She said nothing.

'Are you coming?'

'No.'

He took a deep breath, his fists balled, his shoulders tensed and he leapt towards me. I stepped back and took his arms, twisted him around and pushed him away.

'Enough!' she yelled.

'Not a chance!' he shouted. His legs were shaking, his eyes were popping. Sweat ran down his cheeks and filled his moustache. 'Not a chance,' he repeated, 'no way!', and he turned towards his car. I took a step towards him but Elizabeth stood between us. 'Jacob,' she said. 'Please. Listen to me...'

'No!' He wheeled around. 'You listen to me! I'll tell you!' He pointed at me. 'And I'll tell you. I'm sure you want to know all about Baja...'

'I know about Baja.'

'And Thailand?' He gulped air. 'Goa? How about it? British Columbia?'

Elizabeth said, 'Nothing happened in British Columbia.' She turned away. 'And you weren't in Thailand.'

He nodded at me. 'You know she's a serial back-to-basics freak?' Saliva had accumulated at the corners of his mouth. 'Oh, yeah!' He was raving. 'She could have been one of the greats, she could have been up there, she didn't have to be remembered as the blonde in *Missing You*, but no, she kept meeting guys like you in places like this.'

'I did not keep meeting...'

'Sure you did. Yeah. You kept thinking that the simple life was for you. But you always ended up running home, didn't you, Mother?' He tongued the corners of his mouth. 'You always found something to miss.'

'What do you know?' she said. 'What the hell do you know about what I missed? Or what I wanted?'

'Go,' I said.

'Go?' He laughed.

'Yes.'

He looked at his mother, took a step towards her; she backed away. She held up her hands, palms to the front, and said, 'Leave me alone.' He pointed at me, squinted, grabbed his shoulder and winced. He opened his mouth to say something. I watched his eyes swivel, and his tongue moved, but no sound came out. He looked through me, staring at some spot beyond the ruins. The air froze and split. I waited, Elizabeth waited, but then he turned instead and went to his car. He put on his sunglasses and drove away from Port Juliet at speed, through the potholes without slowing, and we stood and listened until the place was quiet again, and the air calmed.

The air settled, clouds puffed over the sea and the guano on the offshore stacks glowed in the setting sun. The tide laid its cargo along the shore: lumps of wood, weed, empty shells and a plastic bottle. The sand was smooth and spongy. We walked slowly. My arms ached, my back twinged and my knuckles bled. Gloria ran ahead. The cat sat and watched us from the ruins. I picked up a stick. It was shaped like a horse's head.

'I can't deny it,' she said. 'There's truth in what he said. But it was only Baja that made me want to live a quieter life. Those other places, they meant nothing. It was Baja that held me.' She stopped and looked towards the ruins. 'And this place. My mother's place...'

'I shouldn't have hit him.' I rubbed the small of my back. 'I'm getting too old for that sort of thing.'

'He had it coming.'

'I haven't been in a fight for years.' I felt my ribs, and ran the tips of my fingers over my chin. I was cut, but the bleeding had stopped. 'But I couldn't stand and listen to him talk to you like that. You're his mother.'

'That's his problem. He blames me. He might have a point. I was never around for him, not when he needed me, I know that.'

'I wasn't around when my mother needed me. But I didn't treat her like that…'

'Rich children; they're different. They don't have reasons, just excuses. Excuses and blame.'

'What does he do?'

'Do?'

'Does he work?'

She laughed. 'He thinks he does, but he doesn't have to. That's my problem, trying to pay off the guilt with money. It's the way I punish myself for the neglect. My son… he calls himself an actor. Did you ever see *Booth and Bother*?'

'What was it?'

'A sit-com.'

'No.'

'He had a walk-on in that. He was a policeman. Had to walk in on Booth and his girlfriend and tell him that Bother was lost. Bother was a dog.' She shook her head. 'That's the only job he's ever had. He can't walk right, let alone act. People have told him but he's stubborn. He says he's going to make it.'

We had reached the end of the beach, and sat down on the scattered rocks that lay at the foot of the cliff. 'Is he?' I said. A group of oyster-catchers jigged along the tideline, running from the waves, running back to them, poking in the sand, running away again.

'Not a chance.'

'Will he come back?'

'Sure.'

'And will you go?'

She shrugged. 'Maybe he's right. Maybe I always find something to miss, but I still feel I could be all right here, I could

116

get rid of so much shit. Sometimes I think about the orange groves, when I was a kid, and I can smell rain on the blossom, and I think that was the only time I was truly happy. A bowl of soup for lunch, a piece of bread. Living with my mother, living with someone I loved and who loved me back.'

'Unconditional love, that's a great thing. And honest work. Knowing, feeling you've earned your money. Slow drinks, easy evenings. Evenings like this. You don't have to prove anything in a place like this. You just live, and life takes care of itself, doesn't it? Bumper stickers don't come into it.'

'Bumper stickers?'

'Mottos. Aphorisms.'

'They don't come into it if you can afford to ignore them. If you've got the money. Your mother's life didn't take care of itself...'

'No, it didn't. I know. Different times. Hard times, not our times, Michael.'

The way you said my name touched me. My name had never sounded so sweet. I wanted to kiss your hands and say that this was the easiest evening of my life, and that you could take care of your life in my company for as long as you wanted.

I wanted you to say it again, to say that I had showed you something you'd forgotten.

Wanted to say the same, wanted to hear my voice like a bell in my head.

Ringing, not tolling.

Wanted to drown.

Do you remember the oyster-catchers? They were feeding along the beach?

Nervously.

Along the tideline.

'Oh,' I said, but nothing else. My mouth felt full of cotton. I dipped my fingers in a rock pool and touched an anemone. Its fronds tingled, contracted and folded away. A little fish darted

117

away from my shadow, and another. Gloria sat and watched the clifftop. She narrowed her eyes and held her mouth slightly open. Rabbits were coming out to graze the edges and verges. She made a move and the oyster-catchers blew away, darting towards the point, crying and turning over the cliffs and the disappearing rabbits. The dog stood still.

'Aphorisms never mean enough,' she said.

'Stay,' I said.

'One word is all you need.'

'Sometimes. If you need that word. Or want it.'

'Want is different to can, you know that.'

'Yes.'

'I make no promises.'

'Good. Promises shouldn't fail.'

'I'm here this evening. Make that enough, Michael.'

'Okay,' I said. 'It's enough.'

'You said the right thing.'

But I hadn't, not exactly.

16

In 1966 the love of my life took my chin in her hand and said, 'I'm here today, Michael. Make that enough.' At that time in Barcelona I could not. The sun fumed on the city, fountains played and the smell of freshly baked bread floated in the air. My heart stirred in its bed, turned towards the light and opened one eye. Then the other, and I had found what I had lost, and believed I could live for ever. My life changed with one look.

I was thirty-nine, and had taken Captain Perkins's advice. I had lived carefully for two years. I hadn't drunk. I hadn't been with a woman. I earned my mate's ticket. I grew a beard. I read more books than you could pile, novels and biographies, and the histories of places I had visited. Malagasy, Gabon, Kerguelen and the daft islands of the Flores Sea.

The MV *Katia Prelude* sailed from Tilbury in September, carrying coal for Marseille. The Channel blew, Biscay was rough, and the propeller shaft wrenched in a force nine. The sound of screaming metal, forced bolts and wrenched, bleeding bearings... We limped into the Mediterranean, dry-docked for repairs in Barcelona and were stood down.

I took a room in a quiet house in the old part of the city. My room overlooked a courtyard where a fountain played and baskets of flowers hung. Bees flew, cats slept on the cobbles, and the sound of a distant piano drifted in through my window. I sat on the balcony, poured freshly squeezed fruit juice over crushed ice and settled down to read the great novelist Zane Grey.

Do you recognise the person you could spend a life with immediately? Does everyone do this? With one look? Is it like knowing that the sea is deep? That the sea is deep and blue? That fish swim... When she says her name is it confirmed? For ever? Doubt banished? Isabel was the landlord's daughter. She came from a downstairs room, crossed the courtyard and stopped for a moment to dip her fingers in the fountain. She tasted the water, and dribbled some of it across her brow. Then she disappeared, and I heard her climb the stairs to my room. She knocked. I put my book down and went to open the door. She was holding a bucket and mop in one hand, and a basket of cloths and bottles in the other. She said, 'Good morning.' I didn't move. 'I've come to clean your room.' My focus sharpened, and all the things I had denied myself flooded my head. I felt exact. I knew that I was in exactly the right place. It was half past ten in the morning, and birds were singing over the courtyard.

Isabel was a tall woman. She had short black hair. Her mouth was like a fruit. She wore silver studs in her ears, and a pearl necklace. She smelt of lemons. I took a deep breath. She wore red shoes, a black skirt and a red blouse. 'Come in,' I said. She had brown eyes, bird eyes. I stood to one side. She smiled and walked into my room.

It was tidy. The curtains were open and the bed was made. My clothes were neatly folded. She whistled at them, and walked through to the bathroom. She filled her bucket and washed the floor. As she worked she put her head round the door and said, 'I was in London.' Her voice was notes.

'Were you?'

'Three years.'

'Where?'

'Greenwich. My uncle has a restaurant.' She squirted something into the bath, bent over and scrubbed. A curl of hair dropped into her eyes. She touched it away. 'I was in the kitchen.'

I told her I was born on the Isle of Dogs, in a house with a view across the river to Greenwich, and she told me she could do wonderful things with prawns. I said I was staying two weeks. She told me that she would show me the city of Barcelona. For the second time in my life I left a book half finished.

She said, 'I do not like beards.' I shaved mine off. She said, 'I would love to visit Besalú.' We took the bus out of the city and into the hills. Over the old bridge and into the beautiful town. Sitting in a café with a view of the river. A bottle of wine. 'Can I have a glass?' I poured. Later, in the market: 'Can I have an orange?' I bought two kilos. Back in Barcelona: 'I will show you how to cook *zarzuela de mariscos*.' You never tasted food like it. It danced on the plate.

Isabel... She took me to a bar, ordered beer and paid a guitarist to play a song. I was in a trance. I had been waiting for her. I asked her if she had been waiting for me. I had known her a week. 'Maybe,' she said. It was all I needed. I took her hand and told her that I would leave the sea for her. I took off my cap and showed it to her. I showed her my mother's stitching, and the frayed peak. I told her about my father, and Captain Perkins. She shook her head but I nodded mine.

'You cannot leave the sea.'

'I can. I've money saved.'

'Keep it.'

'I don't want to. Not while you're living.'

'The sea is your home.'

'It's my bed, that's all.' I took her hand and promised her anything she wanted. She turned her face away.

How can a face catch a man? How can a look take him to the edge of his feelings and make him think the impossible? Why can eyes be that deep?

'Please,' she said. 'I cannot play games.'

'You think this is a game?' I slapped my forehead.

'What do you call it?'

I wanted to say that I called it the most important thing I had ever decided. If you deny your life the gifts it is due then you can only blame yourself. I wanted to tell Isabel Morago that I would, at her command, rip my heart from my chest and show her its swollen chambers. I would spread my fingers and display the cuts in the palms of my hands. If you don't acknowledge your desires you will live in a swamp of dead wishes, vague memories and imagined pleasures. Nothing but regret. I said, 'I mean it.'

'I'm here today, Michael. Make that enough.'

'How can I?'

'It's what I want. You promised me what I wanted.' Isabel was quick. She missed nothing. 'I want you to be with me now, and I want you to write to me.' She patted my hand. 'I cannot say what will happen.'

I made those six words a talisman. I threaded them in my head and hung them in my heart. I took them to mean whatever I wanted, so when I was in despair I knew they meant we would never meet again, but when I was gay they were her invitation to a lifetime of love. It could happen. We could open a restaurant in the old town, we could have children, we could take holidays in Besalú. 'I cannot say what will happen.' Every promise I ever wanted to hear was locked in those words.

The MV *Katia Prelude* sailed from Barcelona in the second week of October. Isabel waved to me from the dock, and I stood on the bridge wing until Spain smudged, its lights came on and the place failed beneath the horizon. I went below and wrote my first letter to her. I told her that I was a lonely man, that I would learn to be a waiter. I would learn about wine. I wrote about the ship, the captain, the crew and our cargo. I repeated that the sea was not my home, it never could be. I was a sailor by chance. I had been born watching ships; I never gave another life a second thought. Believe me.

I imagined her opening the letter in her room, taking it to the fountain in the courtyard and reading it while the water played and bees came to the flowers that hung from the walls of her father's house. 'How,' I wrote, 'can one memory of you be enough?', and as the words bled from my pen a storm blew off the old country, ripped the sea and took the MV *Katia Prelude* by surprise.

'I cannot say what will happen...', around and around in my head as the ship was lifted one early morning and spun like a top, first port to starboard, then starboard to port. I was in my bunk, I was thinking hard about Isabel, and how much I wanted that café, the one she thought I could never manage. I was thrown out of bed, the door burst open and the mate ordered me up and out. A hatch had loosened. We were shipping water. We had to move.

I remember thinking, and that was my mistake. I thought *I'm afraid* as four of us buckled up. Afraid of that boiling sea but mostly afraid that I would never see Isabel again. I saw her face, I smelt her in the brine, I stuffed my cap inside my shirt and slid along the deck, bounced off the generator vents and into the legs of the man in front of me. He grabbed my collar, pulled me up and said, 'We're not losing you. Lucky,' and when the ship settled between waves, we made a dash for the hatch, roped ourselves to the rail and went to work.

One of the catches had sheared and the others had loosened, so as the sea washed over the deck the hatch was forced wider. We waited for another lull, then jumped on it and began to screw the good catches down. Mine was stiff, the others were easy. I braced myself with my feet, leant back and pulled. It moved an inch, then another inch, the lull broke and the ship began to climb. I looked up and saw the bows rising, and beyond them the top of the wave twenty-five feet above me. I knew what was going to happen. I shouted to the others. Their catches were tight now and they yelled, 'Let's go!'

'Lucky!'

'Go!'

They untied and ran without looking back, up the deck to the generator house. I saw them go inside, and stand to watch me struggle with my rope. It wouldn't untie; the ship reached the apex and all I saw was sky. I felt for my cap, I crushed it against my skin and closed my eyes. The air wailed around me, we lurched madly, hung for seconds... and dropped. I covered my head, curled as tightly as I could and waited. I heard the other men shout, I heard the wave burst over the bridge, and a groan of steel. A rail buckled, snapped and clattered across the deck and then I was hit, smashed down by a ton of water and balled against the edge of the hatch.

I remember thinking again, thinking as I filled with water, *I am not going to die, but I'll lose an arm. Or a leg. Or my sense. My sense of colour. My sight.* Everything was black. I yelled, spat, felt blood in my mouth and the taste of steel. The lull came and a moment of silence I must have imagined, and then the others were coming back for me, sliding down the deck. I opened my eyes and they looked as though they were moving

in a dream. Their faces were grey. The ship slewed and began
to climb the next wave.

The deck moaned, I stood up, the men were with me. The
ocean rose behind them, building walls and floors, adding a
roof, steaming from every edge. The men, they looked too
small. I tried to speak but blood bubbled the words. I saw a
hand move in front of my face. It was holding a knife. The
knife came down behind me, the rope was cut and arms were
lifting me up. I was pulled, dragged, I held my head and yelled.
Blood flew. 'Shut it!' one shouted, and I did. I clutched inside
my shirt, I crushed my cap, I pinched my skin. The ship began
to crest and lurch. I heard 'Got him?' and then I was up and
into a dark place, the generator house, and into the companionway that ran to the galley, and a dry floor. A dry floor, a
warm place by the ovens, the love of my life and bruised ribs.
I was a strong man. I would live, but how?

I asked Elizabeth, 'Who was the love of your life? Did you
have one?'

'The love of my life... You're meant to have one, aren't you?'

'Of course.'

'The love of my life... You had one?'

'Yes.'

'Who was she?'

'Isabel Morago.'

We were driving to Zennack to see if Jacob had stayed the
night at Mrs Bell's, or if Dan had heard something in the pub,
or if Mr Boundy had overheard an agitated telephone conver-
sation. Elizabeth sat on the wheel arch, one foot on the back
of the seat, the other on the link-box. We had to shout. 'Jim
Vesala was the love of my life. Poor guy...'

'What happened?'

'He didn't make it.'

'Make what?'

She laughed. 'God, I love the way you talk!'

'I can't help it.'

'He didn't make it as an actor…'

'I never heard of him.'

'Heard of *The Black Stones*?'

'Yes.'

'He was in that.'

'I think I saw it…'

'It bombed, but he was a good man. That was his problem. Too good for the business. A beautiful man. He had healing hands. A child's hands… A child's mind.' She looked towards the sea and sighed. 'He shot himself.'

'I'm sorry.'

'Why?'

The day was high and blue, no clouds, spring. The curtains along the road twitched, and the larks rose. The air was sweet; lambs ran to their mothers. 'People shouldn't deny themselves this.'

'I agree,' she said.

'Why did he do it?'

'Because he couldn't stand failing.'

'But he made you happy?'

'Yeah. That was the tragedy. He didn't realise that he did one thing so well, that he hadn't failed. Or maybe he did and just needed telling. I should have told him. I was so dumb.' She tapped my shoulder. 'One thing's all you need, but you have to recognise it. Love it and use it, Michael. We've got that in common.'

'Have we?'

'Sure,' she said. 'Absolutely.'

'We don't need to have anything in common.'

'That's a strange thing to say.'

'What did you have in common with Jim Vesala?'

'Need.'

Isabel and I had our letters in common. When we wrote we were passionate, desperate. Our lives depended on the words we wrote. I would write, 'I love the sea, but it is nothing compared to you. You are deeper than it,' and she would reply, 'I love all the things you say, and maybe I believe them. I sometimes think about our little restaurant. I was in the old town today and saw a place that would be perfect, and I imagined you standing by the door with a napkin over your arm. My uncle used to do that.'

I wrote from Marseille, 'The further I am from you the more I love you,' and she replied, 'Does this mean that if I am lying in your arms you will love me less than you do now?'

I replied: 'I love you, Isabel, I love you more than I have ever loved anyone.'

She wrote: 'I believe you, Michael.'

Our tragedy: when we met again we didn't mention the letters we had written. We behaved as though we were seeing each other for the first time, and the letters were something we had imagined. Neither of us could talk about the things we had written. We sat and drank and held hands in a bar on the waterfront; I wanted to say so much but said nothing but the banal. I watched her lips move, and the tongue inside her mouth. She wore a flower in her hair, and sandals on her feet. I had twenty-four hours ashore, then home to Tilbury. I was locked in need, but could not ask her if she felt the same.

'Need,' said Elizabeth, 'is a terrible thing.'

Mrs Bell told us that Jacob had passed through in the night, and stopped to book a room for Sunday. 'Or two nights. He wasn't sure. I told him I couldn't reserve a bed if he wasn't sure he wanted it, it wasn't fair on me, so he put a deposit on two. Cash. He seemed quite charming.' She didn't take her eyes off Elizabeth's clothes. She was using her scarf as a belt, her blouse as a vest and one of my check shirts as a jacket, a pair of my shrunk cord trousers tucked into a pair of boots with newspaper stuffed into the toes and a clean white handkerchief tied around her neck. She looked comfortable and chic. Her hair was tied in a bun. She laughed.

Mrs Bell frowned and said, 'He used my bathroom. He was in quite a state. Cut face, bleeding knees. He could hardly see out of one of his eyes. Said he'd fallen over.'

'He slipped on the rocks,' I said.

Mrs Bell shook her head. 'I'm not surprised. Wearing shoes like that. Leather soles.'

'And you say he was charming?' said Elizabeth.

'Perfectly.'

Elizabeth laughed. 'He can be.'

Mrs Bell was standing on the doorstep. We were standing on the garden path. She took a step towards me so she was closer to me than Elizabeth was, and said, 'He seemed very worried.'

'About what?' said Elizabeth.

'The situation.'

'The situation? You make it sound like an army manoeuvre.'

'I think,' said Mrs Bell, firmly now, 'that he was only doing what any concerned son would do.'

'Concerned son?' Elizabeth nodded. 'Sure. Concerned about his pocket book. He doesn't give a fuck about me...'

Mrs Bell's face flushed with blood, and her hands fisted. She said, 'There's no need for language.'

'Language?'

'You know what I mean.'

'Language?'

Mrs Bell folded her arms now, and for a moment the air snapped. I took a deep breath and said, 'He's coming back on Sunday?'

'I'll be happy to have him,' said Mrs Bell. 'More than happy...'

Elizabeth turned away and walked down the garden path. 'Language?' she said, and she crossed the square to the post office.

'Really,' said Mrs Bell.

'He's not such a nice person...'

'But he's her son!'

'And her problem,' I said.

Mrs Bell shrugged. She does not have children of her own. She said, 'Are we still going to the cinema tomorrow?'

'Of course. I'll come over about five.'

'I'm looking forward to it.' Mrs Bell fluttered her hands, and for a moment I thought she was going to touch me, but then she turned and went back to her house. 'Five?' she said.

'I'll be here.'

17

Doomed love can kill. I knew a man who died because a woman did not love him. Jack was from Brighton, a small man with curly blond hair and bulbous eyes. He always wore a shirt and tie, and worked as wireless operator on the MV *Frelon Brun*, a tanker. He met her in Rio de Janeiro, and he should not have done that.

It was bar, a drink, a flight of lamplit stairs and a slip. It was him not understanding that they had trade in common. A service. It had nothing to do with love but Jack didn't know that. He was a young man, it was only his second voyage, the drinks were strong. His hair was admired and the women of Rio are very beautiful.

Maybe it was the heat. When you sail you don't notice it creeping up on you. You leave the northern waters, the skies lighten, the air smells of spice, not herb. Ripening berries, not leaves. Your eyes water; love is possible for anyone.

Jack met Anna in a bar and she was so willing, so quick and slow. He had never met a woman like her, and thought that she meant it, that she wanted to wrap her bare legs around his waist because she loved him. He told all about her, and I knew what he was talking about, I knew what a woman's skin did. He was so far from home, and his work kept him in a room all day, listening on the headset to people he had never met and never would. Voices changed by ether, his voice crackling back. He thought so much about his mother and father, and his sister. He wondered if he had chosen the right life; Anna told him that he had, and that he was so good, so kind.

Jack jumped ship and disappeared into Rio, chasing Anna to nowhere, I suppose. It is easy to imagine what happens to a man like him, but difficult to tell. The inevitable is written on some people's faces. Maybe it is better to dream and die young.

Jack Potter in Rio de Janeiro, standing on a street corner, midnight. Looking up at a window, seeing his love's silhouette, biting his lip. I don't know what happened, but this is how I see him. Chasing a woman he could never have, never understanding his folly, dreaming of skin, taking a knife in the side, dying thousands of miles from home with a stranger's name on his lips. His hair flopped over his eyes, his hand bent back at an unnatural angle. His watch gone. This is how I see him.

I did not let love for Isabel kill me, even after she wrote to tell me about Bernardo Roderada from Sant Feliu de Guixols. She had met him at a party. She didn't say much but I could see him: handsome, white shirt, partnership in his father's bar. I could see her: sitting on her balcony, holding a postcard of Sant Feliu in one hand and a glass of wine in the other. A smile on her face. I saw them walking together on Las Ramblas, in the mountains, beside a lake, along the shore. I saw her losing any memory she had of me. I saw their fingers touching.

I was not her type and I would never convince her that I could leave the sea. I was not a slim man with thick hair and a taste for well-tailored clothes. Sometimes I drank too much, and I had melancholy moods. And sometimes we didn't meet for months. These were the reasons she preferred Bernardo Roderada to me, and they were good reasons too. I couldn't deny them. Ask any sailor.

I lit the lamps, stoked the fire and cooked eggs. We sat at the kitchen table to eat. The night was clear and sparkled with cold. Elizabeth gave me a sly look and told me that Mrs Bell was sweet on me. 'She was giving you some looks.'

I said, 'Don't be ridiculous. She's not my type.'

'Maybe you're hers.'

'Forget it.'

'She wants you, Michael. Believe me.'

'We're friends, that's all.'

'Tell me that when you get back from the cinema. What are you seeing?'

'*Raintown.*'

'Oh, God.'

'What's the matter?' I poured some whisky. 'Is it that bad?'

'No, no,' she said, quietly. 'I think it's the best thing I've done. It might make me a star again.'

'Once a star, always a star. You know that. It's in your face, your eyes.'

'The camera loves them?'

'Exactly.'

'You wouldn't have said that a few years back. Not if you'd seen me.'

'What was the problem?'

'You know...' She spread her arms, tipped her head back and laughed at the ceiling. 'End-of-the-line stuff. Some days... some days I wouldn't even get out of bed. When you've seen what could be, then watched what could be disappear... I was a lonely woman for years, Michael. Lonely as hell. That's why Jacob... why he's so sickening. He didn't care, not for years, not until he caught the scent of money. Let me tell you; if Bob Mitchum hadn't put my name up for *Raintown*, God knows, I wouldn't be talking to you now. That man's one in a million. The movie's one in a million.' She cleared her throat with some whisky, and smiled. 'But hey... I'm not going to say any more about it. You tell me what you think tomorrow. After the credits have run and the lights are up. And I want the truth, no bullshit just to keep me happy. I can tell. I used to know people who never had a bad word for my work. I suppose they didn't want to upset me, but they didn't have the sense to understand that not wanting to do that was the worst thing they could do.'

'Okay.'

One of the lamps flared. I adjusted the flame, and she said, 'When you go to the movies, do you sit through the credits?'

'Yes.'

'I thought so.'

'Why?'

She drank. 'I was thinking that this place is like the credits. The movie's over but it's just beginning in your head. You're seeing it again, but differently, and you can watch it for as long as you like. You're alone in the cinema, except you're not. There's always one other person sitting ten rows away.'

'What are you talking about?'

'I know what I mean, but I don't know how to explain it. Not yet, anyway.' She finished her eggs and pushed her plate away.

'You're tired.'

She looked at her watch. 'I wonder how many people will stay to watch the credits tonight.'

'Who knows?'

'Who cares?'

I picked up the bottle. 'Drink?'

'Sure.'

131

I poured. 'Enough?'

She nodded and said, 'Did you ever have an affair with some-one you couldn't be with? One of those things where you had to sneak around. Catch a look here, a kiss there. An hour in some bar you wouldn't normally be seen dead in, trying to find the right words. Telling each other if only, and asking why time is so cruel.'

'I think so.'

'You either did or didn't.'

'I did,' I said. 'Once...'

'Okay...'

'Why?'

'Why... Well, did you promise that person that one day, when you were both older, you'd meet again, and you'd take a vacation together, and the past would be forgotten? Some romantic hotel in the mountains and you'd live like you were meant to. No fear. No guilt. No regrets. No wondering if a face you knew was waiting around the next corner. You'd walk for miles and tell each other your secrets but they wouldn't matter. The time for secrets would be past. You could say exactly what you wanted, when you wanted, how you wanted. You'd be too old to care about anything but her. You'd live like a story you read when you didn't know better.'

'I don't remember.'

'You remember, Michael. She was perfect for you, she had a face you could steal, but she had another man waiting for her. And he'd be waiting for you if he knew. Tell me...'

'What?'

'What was her husband's name?'

I shrugged. 'He was Greek. Piraeus.'

'What happened?'

'It was like you said. We used to walk to where the fishing boats were pulled up on the shingle. I told her I was going to buy one of them and we'd sail away in it. We'd find an island, spend our time fishing. But that was a dream. We knew it. Nothing but dreams.'

'They're my trade.'

'You had affairs?'

Now she laughed. 'I was an affair.' She drank. 'And I heard that promise so many times, and I made it too. It never comes true, not the way you expect.'

'What does that mean?'

'You know what it means,' she said, and she lit a cigarette. 'Don't you?'

I did not deny it. I poured more drink.

'I don't think I was ever loved, not since my mother died. Jim tried, but then I didn't notice. I was so stupid...'

I said, 'Me too. More than I knew. I thought I loved a woman but I was using her. I didn't have a clue. Not back then. I was blind.'

'That was Isabel?'

'That was Isabel,' I said, 'a long time ago,' and for a second I wanted to say that I wasn't stupid any more, that I could love and she could believe me, but I kept quiet. I picked up the bottle and poured again in my house.

18

Is regret a disease? Does distance give it strength? Can it become a pleasure? Can regret become stronger than love, and overtake its reason?

I never stopped wanting Isabel, even after she married Bernardo Roderada and moved to Sant Feliu de Guixols. She worked in her husband's bar, waiting at table. The sun was hot, the breeze warm, the rain soft as paint, but who cared? Did the birds that flocked to sing in the trees, or the old men who carried boxes of fruit along the promenade? Did the priest care, as he strolled to visit a sick woman? Isabel did not, and she did not doubt, but I knew that loss is the worst kiss.

It should have been me: I began to indulge in a perfect murder fantasy. The crime of passion, a man lying in a pool of blood and guts at the foot of the cliffs that climb to the south of the town: yes, I have taken the early bus to Sant Feliu de Guixols. I have stood under the trees that grow along the promenade. I have turned my collar up to watch her working. I have seen the handsome Bernardo standing at the door with a white napkin over his arm, and I have seen him put his arm around her waist and kiss her lips. It should have been me, but I have to get back to my loaded ship. It should have been me, but I am standing in this Spanish drizzle watching her sweep the pavement after closing time, stopping to lean on the handle and wipe her brow. It should have been me, but I could not give her the grief of a dead husband. I know that much. I know I love her that much. It should have been me holding her in a wide bed in the room at the back, but I am sleeping on the beach with the dogs of the town. They are sniffing my feet and licking my face. The first bus leaves early in the morning.

Two days later I was lost at sea. I knew where the ship was. I knew its exact position. I stood on watch and counted the degrees and minutes but did not know where my heart was. It drifted, rudderless, windless. My thoughts concentrated on Isabel and why I had not made her happy. Had I fought in her presence? Had I forgotten to write one week? Had I ignored her father? Had I not proved that I could live without the sea? That I had money saved?

Maybe she didn't believe me. Maybe she never trusted me. Maybe the things I said were lost in translation. The love of your life marries and life goes on. Flowers do not die, rivers continue to flow, every day has a night. The tectonic plates do not split and the sea does not drain away. God does not appear and display his chest. He does not speak. He does not prove that we are a part of a master plan. We are not in step with the stars. This is the worst of it. Something so important affects nothing; love can leave no mark. That is the crime.

The sea sleeps, but not necessarily at night. It always wakes with a new face. I watched it open its eyes as I stood on a middle watch. The sky was the black blanket wrenched from its face. A wind blew from the east and the waves began to crest. I pulled the hood of my coat over my head and buttoned up. Ahead of the ship the sea was frothing and wrenching itself in desperate heaves; we hit a trough. Slammed through. Hit another. Slammed twice. The navigation lights dimmed. The engines wailed and the captain called me in from the wing.

The bridge was warm but I was cold inside. Failed. I watched the storm through the glass. The ship was strong, the captain was called Morrison and believed that Jesus Christ was the Risen Saviour, and loved and watched over our every move. I tried to understand but could not.

'Say a prayer. Number One,' he barked. He was standing with his legs planted, his arms folded. I said, 'Aye, aye, sir,' and tried to remember one.

A minute passed. I felt blank.

'Said it, Number One?'

Blank.

'Number One?'

'Sir?'

'Trust the prayer was a good one.' He didn't take his eyes off the sea ahead.

'It was what the situation demanded, sir.'

'God heard you, Number One.'

'I hope so...'

'Believe me.' He gave me a stern look. 'And that's an order.'

Elizabeth and I got up early in the morning, walked down to the shore and swam, and when we were there I thought again *It could have been me.* Is it romance that makes me think this way, or desire? I saw the world, I never wanted wealth, I live in the place of my dreams. The offshore stacks shine, the sun is warming for the day, there is Gloria sitting on the beach, guarding the towels, and the cat is hiding in the ruins of the weavers' cottages.

The water was cold but as we swam my blood warmed, my legs were strong, my muscles didn't cramp, I took easy strokes. She was watching me, and I watched her. She swam easily and I swam towards her.

When we met she didn't stop, she carried on kicking and spreading her arms and we swept into each other. I felt her feet on mine. She grabbed my shoulders and pushed me down. I swallowed water, hit the bottom and pushed up. As I did I reached out and touched her waist. She yelled. I surfaced, pushed down on her head, she went down and I kicked away from her. I turned on my back and floated. She came up beneath me, grabbed my ankles and pulled down. I shouted and flipped over. She let go and bobbed up in front of me. I stared into her eyes and she stared back at me. I remembered the look and the feeling, and I was not as old as I thought I was. The impossible was as possible as it used to be, as it used to be in Barcelona in 1966. I was sixty-eight years old and Elizabeth Green was seventy-five years old. Is that too old, or do we just become lazy? I took her face in my hands and said, 'Look…'

'No,' she said. 'You look.' Serious as hell. 'I can't play games.'

'You think this is a game?' I moved away from her.

'What do you call it?'

'You can only blame yourself if you deny life. Desire's a good thing. Regret I can live without.'

'What do you want, Michael?'

'This moment, that's all.'

'I want more than that,' she said, and before I could speak, before I could tell her that she was contradicting herself, she reached for my arm, pulled me to her and kissed my lips.

It is the dream I had in the Bay of Bengal, the Tasman Sea and the Panama Canal. Over the Grand Banks and off the Angolan coast. The Chagos Archipelago. The Aleutian Islands. In fog banks, in seas the size of evil and over seas like glass. In rooms over bars in Rio and Hamburg with a girl who knew a navigation officer called Jurgen and did I know him. Or I was in Tilbury and I was leaving the Gaumont. I'd just seen *Missing You* for the eighth time, and I was watching the final scenes in my head as I was jostled in the crowd, out of the warm and on to the pavement. But not a pavement in Tilbury; I was in Marseille, and I could see her through the cafe window, except now there was no one waiting for her, George really was dead in the desert, and she needed someone to turn to.

'Michael?'

I had your face in my hands. You were mine; the million other people who said they loved you were lying. When you kissed Cary Grant it meant nothing to you. You were not a movie star. You were bigger than that and your mouth tasted of salt and vodka.

We were very chaste. We did not open our mouths or move our hands away from our faces and shoulders. The sea swelled towards us, and as we relaxed she fell on to me. We sank, broke and came up again, and she splashed towards the shore, stood in the shallows and waded to the towels. Gloria barked. I lay back and floated again. A cloud drifted by, and then another. High cirrus. It was about half past nine, and we hadn't eaten breakfast.

She cooked pancakes and I felt bold enough to put my feet up and ask, 'What more do you want?'

She didn't answer.

'Are you going home with Jacob?'

She flipped the first pancake and said, 'You want this one?'

'He's coming tomorrow, you...'

'Please!' She slammed the frying pan down. 'I know when they're coming!'

'Them? Who's them?'

'He'll bring Angie with him.' She slid the pancake on to a plate. 'My agent,' she said, and poured some more mixture into the pan.

'Why?'

'She'll remind me about my commitments and what I'll lose if I renege. She'll call me selfish, sympathise with Jacob. He's the advance party. She's the big guns.'

The pancake was very good. I squeezed lemon juice over it. 'What are your commitments?'

She did not answer straight away. She fiddled with the pan, turning it this way and that. Gloria sat up to watch, her mouth open, panting. I put some of my pancake in my mouth and chewed. 'Pieces of paper,' she said.

'What does that mean?'

She slid her pancake on to a plate and came to the table. She sat down opposite me and sighed. 'I've got the lead in another movie,' she said. 'And if you knew how difficult it is for a seventy-five-year-old woman in Hollywood...'

'I can imagine.'

'And then there's the money. I'm being offered more money for ten weeks' work than I earned in thirty years.' She smiled. 'But the most important thing is being wanted. Needed. People who used to leave the room when I walked in return my calls. When I signed that contract...'

'You're wanted with or without a contract. You know that.'

'Sure. But do I believe it?'

'Don't ask me.'

'You said the right thing again.'

'I've had a lot of practice.'

'So it's automatic? Maybe you don't mean it.'

'I mean it all right,' I said.

In the afternoon we walked down to the weavers' cottages. The sun was bright. Solitary clouds drifted as slow as our walking, their shadows following the feathering of the grass in the fields.

We wandered through the ruins. Weeds were growing where the floors had been, and tufts of grass sprouted from the cracked window sills. Elizabeth stopped to pick up a shard of broken glass, wiped it on her sleeve, held it to her eye and said, 'My mother could have looked through this.'

I said, 'I wonder which cottage was hers.'

Elizabeth narrowed her eyes and nodded her head, slowly. 'This one. This was it.' It was the second along in the row of five, and she was certain. 'I can see her here.' She looked at the broken walls, the piles of stone, a blackened hole where a fireplace had been. Her eyes were glazed and red. 'She made cloth for a tailor in town. Zennack, I suppose.'

'Or Truro,' I said, uselessly.

'Or Truro,' she repeated, softly, an echo, and she took my arm. 'She told me she never wanted to leave a place so much. And then, later, want to return to a place so much. She missed this ocean.' She looked at the sky. 'And the light.'

'A painter used to live here, a long time ago.'

'Yeah?'

'For the light.'

We stepped over a low pile of shattered slate, through the gap where the front door had been and into the overgrown waste of the gardens. These sloped to a broken wall, some strands of rusted wire and the beach. A cloud shaped over the offshore stacks, dying as the high breezes ripped its edges, and then its heart.

'She used to sit here and watch the sun go down. Used to wait for my father to come home and kick her around the block.'

I looked at the ground.

'Would you fetch some chairs?'

'Of course.'

139

She squeezed my arm.

I patted her hand and broke away. 'Don't go away,' I said, and I walked back through the old gardens to my house. As I turned the corner I looked back and watched her for a moment. She was untying her hair, letting it fall over her shoulders. She shook her head and it streamed out, and she ran her fingers through it. She looked towards me and waved. I waved like the boy caught in the bushes, and then went to my house and the kitchen chairs.

19

Cinemas smell the same wherever you are: Singapore, San Francisco, Manila, Truro. Sweet and sour, sticky and human. I did not want to be with Mrs Bell but I could not disappoint her. In the car she had touched my sleeve twice, and as we took our seats, she touched it again. 'Isn't this exciting?' she said. 'I feel like a little girl again.' She was looking around like a girl, one hand rustling a bag of sweets, prattling. 'I remember Father used to take us to the cinema. He called them the flicks. I don't think he enjoyed them, he thought they were irreligious, but he knew we liked to go so that made it all right.'

I had left Elizabeth sitting outside on an indoor chair, staring at the sea from her mother's cottage, and as I drove away, her face clinched my heart. Her eyes, her mouth, cheeks and chin: she wore a look of contentment, the one I wore when I found Port Juliet. A stranger, coming down the road with a hat on his head and seeing her there, would have thought that she was an old resident, maybe the last resident. Someone who knew all there was to know but didn't care. Someone who never asked questions or sucked sweets in the cinema. 'Enjoy it!' she called, and for a moment I was fooled into wondering if she had seen it. Her hair blew, and I wanted to stop the tractor, get down and run to her, but I didn't. You can see a film any time you want, but a promise is a promise. A promise should not fail.

Raintown.

The film opens in Isle of Palms, Florida.

Heat. Sky. Water. Mrs Bell's first sweet. She popped it in her mouth and sucked.

Elizabeth's character (Jennifer) is the ageing owner of a roadside diner, 'BEE HE RT'S'. The 'F' and 'A' on the neon sign are missing.

One day she gets a call from Philadelphia. Her son has been knocked down by a car, and lies critically injured in hospital.

Jennifer takes off her apron. Mrs Bell stopped sucking and crunched. Two hours later Jennifer is boarding a bus for the journey north.

Robert Mitchum plays Al, who boards the bus at the next stop. As he makes his way to the seat opposite Jennifer's, we recognise the eyes of a hard and dangerous man. A man who packs attitude and rage. He takes off his hat, and sits and stares straight ahead. His eyelids are like a lizard's, and his stubble shines. Jennifer holds her bag to her chest, closes her eyes and tries to sleep. Mrs Bell turned to me and said, 'Makes you shiver, doesn't he?'

I hate that. I hate that more than eating sweets in the cinema. It's so rude and I wanted to tell her. Don't talk to me while I'm watching a film. Don't interrupt my concentration. Don't crack me back to real life. Do not break the spell. And Mrs Bell smelt of violets. Elizabeth would never smell of violets. I wanted to be rude back, I wanted to move to a seat on my own but all I did was put my finger to my lips. 'Oh, sorry,' she said, and she went for another sweet.

Night shots: passing coach, heads resting against glass, a bird on a pole.

Morning.

Squinting eyes. Al is holding Jennifer's purse. She wakes, sees it and angrily snatches it back. He protests. It had fallen on the floor. He had picked it up, and was looking after it for her. Honestly. She believes him, and apologises.

A comfort stop at a roadside restaurant. Al plays the perfect gentleman. He shows Jennifer to a corner table and insists on buying her breakfast. She accepts. He doesn't eat. He drinks coffee, and when he picks up the bill, we notice he has plenty of money in his pocket.

We shiver.

Back on the bus.

Crunch.

A glimpse of the driver's newspaper, and a story at the bottom of page six. '*State Police Hunt Murderer. Widow Spencer, 85-year-old Isle of Palms resident, was stayed in what police are describing as "a robbery that went fatally wrong…"* '

Al and Jennifer sit together. They talk about children. She tells him why she is travelling to Philadelphia. He is travelling to Philadelphia too. He is going to visit his mother's grave, something he does every year on the anniversary of her death. The dutiful son.

Jennifer has a nap. He offers his shoulder as a pillow, and she accepts gratefully. Suddenly he is a nice man. He daydreams but never closes his eyes. Mrs Bell took a deep breath.

Another comfort stop, and he buys lunch. When she talks about her injured son, he is so understanding, such a comfort. She takes his arm as they walk back to the coach.

Night follows day, and arrival in Philadelphia. Rain pours. Al and Jennifer part company, but he makes her promise to meet him the following day.

Hospital scene. Intensive care. Jennifer doesn't recognise her son, Jim. He is in a coma, swathed in bandages, fully piped up. Machines beep. She sits for an hour, then leaves for a hotel.

A seedy hotel. Jennifer sits alone while people in the next room shout and fight. Rain beats against the window. She tries to sleep, but cannot.

Morning. She checks out and takes a cab to meet Al in a restaurant. When she tells him about her disturbed night, he promises to find her a quiet hotel. He tells her to meet him in a downtown bar. He writes the address on a card, and gives it to her.

Hospital. Jim is no better. The machines beep. Crunch.

Jennifer walks alone through the streets. Rain pours. Umbrellas bloom. She shelters in a doorway. She reads the address Al gave her.

Al is drinking in a bar, a comfortable one. Jennifer enters. All greets her, they drink together. He is a great comfort. They leave together. He takes her to a hotel, books her into a room next to his. She is so grateful, and takes a long bath.

Al sits alone, a wreath on the bed beside him. His eyes stare, he cannot blink. He notices a speck on his sleeve, and brushes it off. Mrs Bell shivered, rustled and touched my hand. I pulled my hand away. I really couldn't stand it.

Jennifer out of the bath. She phones home, and talks to Betty, a work colleague. Betty tells her that the police have an important lead in the hunt for the widow-slayer. There are no details, but the police are quietly confident.

Jennifer in bed. Al in the corridor outside. His hand on her doorknob. Her phone rings. It's the hospital. Could she come in straight away?

Al retreats; Jennifer dresses and leaves the hotel. Al follows, hailing a cab.

Rain.

Crunch.

Al in the cab, reading a newspaper. The headline 'New Clues: Isle of Palms Widow Slaying'. The police have changed the emphasis of their investigation. Robbery has been discounted as a motive. A witness reports hearing a heated argument, china flying and an old woman (definitely not the victim) leaving the house. When?

An hour or so before the body was found.

Hospital. Jim has recovered from coma. Jennifer holds his hand. He opens his mouth, but cannot speak. Al hovers in the background.

Leaving hospital, a pair of policemen in the hospital reception watch Al as he passes. He puts his hat on and stares straight ahead.

Hotel. Jennifer goes to bed. Al sees her to her room, then leaves the hotel, hails another taxi and disappears into the dawn.

Jennifer sleeps late.

Rustle.

Jennifer wakes, showers, dresses, goes downstairs. Al is waiting in reception. 'How is your son?'

'Better. Much better. I have to go home today.'

'Me too. On the bus?'

Crunch, and Mrs Bell is lucky that I'm a tolerant man.

'Yes.'

'Coincidence,' he says, 'or just my good luck?'

'Luck's just an excuse,' she says.

He nods, and then they leave the hotel together. He stops to buy a newspaper. Headline. '*Police Catch Isle of Palms Widow Killer.*'

Steam rises from the road, the camera climbs and climbs and a panorama of the city spreads below us. Rain falls but it does not bother Jennifer or Al. They wait for a car to pass down the street, then cross and begin to walk away from us. She takes his arm. They remain in the middle of the shot, getting smaller and smaller and smaller until the credits begin to run, their backs are dots in the street and the music swells.

Mrs Bell was out of her seat, buttoning her coat, sucking another sweet and making smacking sounds with her lips. She looked down at me but I wasn't moving. Al had turned to say something to Jennifer, who tipped her head back and smiled. That smile. I knew it. Then a laugh, and I knew that too. Robert Mitchum's face threatened to collapse in love, and she stood ready to catch it. Deeper music and Mrs Bell leaned towards me to say something but I put a finger to my lips and said, 'I'm watching to the end.' I could still see Jennifer and Al.

She looked at the screen. 'But this is the end.'

'Not quite,' I said.

She looked at the screen, then at me, then brushed the front of her coat and huffed. 'I think I'll visit the ladies',' she said. The music soared and pounded. I didn't move. My feet were glowing, and my cheeks. She turned to go. I said, 'I'll meet you outside.' She crunched and I let the music fill me. She waited one more moment, huffed again and left me alone.

As we walked away from the cinema, Mrs Bell blew her nose and talked. I wanted her to be quiet but she did not stop.

She hadn't liked the way the red herring of the widow's murder had kept her on edge, but she'd been pleased that the old couple had found romance together. 'There's no reason why old people shouldn't form attachments, is there?'

'No,' I said.

She drove slowly through the dark, away from Truro to Camborne and the coast road. I was thinking that *Raintown* was the best film I had seen for years, and the best film Elizabeth had made. *Missing You* was good, but *Raintown's* simple story and the understated acting took it out of the ordinary. Mrs Bell said, 'I'd love to go again.'

'Would you?'

'Oh, yes. I see *The Crying Game's* on next week. It sounds quite romantic.'

'I'm sure it is,' I said, but I didn't care. I wanted to get home. I wanted to stoke the fire and sit next to a woman who did not smell of violets, whose voice did not rattle around my head. Mrs Bell was a kind woman and I think she wanted to cook me a meal and mend my shirts.

'Shall we go again?' she said.

'I don't know...'

'Are you all right?' She leaned towards me. Her face was close to me in the car, and I could feel the dryness coming off her. The road was desperate and dark. I watched the stars course, and the gibbous moon.

'Yes.'

'It was strange, wasn't it?'

'What?' I said.

'Seeing her like that. You wouldn't have thought she was the same woman. She looked quite beautiful.'

I wanted to say that I had seen her looking more beautiful, that we had been swimming that morning, that the camera did not do her justice, that her skin smelt of cardamom and jasmine, that her lips tasted of music, but I said 'Yes' instead, and left it like that.

20

I hung my cap on its hook and my coat over the back of a chair, stoked the fire and poured a glass of whisky. Elizabeth sat with a vodka in one hand and a novel by John Buchan in the other. She had tucked one foot up and draped a navy blue blanket around her shoulders. The fire blew out a clot of smoke that broke and danced in streams around the room. I stepped over the dog, joined her on the couch and said, 'What can I say?'

'Don't say anything.'

'It's a great film.'

146

'I told you. Please.' She meant it. 'Don't say anything. Not a word.' She looked at me and smiled. Her teeth were different in real life. They were stained and her lips crept over them. They reflected the lamplight, and spit glistened in their gaps. I could see the veins in her cheeks, and her nose. She straightened her blanket, tapped her book and went back to reading.

I remembered the teeth of a gale in the mad Norwegian Basin. Ice floes, seas the size of any building you want. Stare at them and weep the tears you waited years to shed. You can be trapped in ice but you always break free in the end. Any ship, any heart. Warmth does it. I tried to believe that but it was hard in those waters. I remember leading a gang of men to chip ice from the spars and the deck rails, I remember sending one below when his snot froze and his fingers turned blue. Blue as a baby's eyes, sweet as a baby's smile. The ice calmed the storm but the gale blew on, and chunks of solid wind smashed the hull. The clouds grew mad and tragic over our heads, and shaped themselves like false signals, bad directions to screwed places that no longer exist.

'Elizabeth?'

She tapped the page and said, 'Not till I've finished this chapter.' Her eyebrows were arched. 'Please, Michael.'

'Sorry.'

'Forget it.'

I read over her shoulder for a moment: '*The house, as seen in the half-light, was a long whitewashed cottage, rising to two storeys in the centre. It was plentifully covered with creepers and roses...*', but she clicked her tongue against the roof of her mouth and turned the book away from me. 'And that's very rude,' she said. I hung my head in mock shame.

We sat together. The lamps burned softly, the fire crackled, the pages turned. I let my whisky warm in the glass, and I let good luck swill round my head. Elizabeth twirled strands of hair around her finger. Her skin was creased like old paint and as I looked at her I felt a tightening in my chest and a blurring of vision. The lamplight dulled, and the shadows on the walls faded. Her smell sharpened; it sharpened like a blade, and traced its edge around my eyes. I rubbed them and slid a hand inside my shirt. I could feel my heart beating in there, going like it was about to burst or flood or rage or whine. I took a deep breath, and let it out noisily. She looked at me, touched my shoulder and said, 'I'll be finished in a minute.'

'It's okay.'

She tapped the novel. 'It's exciting.'

'I read it a long time ago,' and my heart missed a beat. 'A long time ago,' I said.

I lived in my own silence after Isabel. I didn't mess up again but returned to earlier, straighter days. Hard work, navigation examinations, moderate drink, strong novels about men under duress and women in rude health. Steamed vegetables and plenty of fish. No women, a tidy cabin, loose underwear and myself in hand. No thought of redemption through violence. A calm voice, a steady stare. The silence of a mind that knows limits. These were the important things in my life at that time.

But silence is not a natural state. It demands its own release. It has a price. As I held the throbbing skin over my heart, and the hairs there curled around my fingers, I was thinking that the noise of the sea was the noise of the ventricles of my body and the uncoiling of my veins. I was watching Elizabeth read by candlelight and my mind was flirting with her as the light on her cheek.

'*The Thirty-Nine Steps*,' I said.

'Ssh.'

'Sorry.'

'Gimme five minutes.'

'I'll give you whatever you want. Whatever takes your fancy. Your fancy's mine, Elizabeth Green.'

'Hush, Michael.'

After the gale we turned at the North Cape and steamed into the Barents Sea, and the ocean thickened and calmed. We were racing to catch a berth but the temperature dropped a final ten degrees and we were trapped, frozen in off Murmansk, anchored in the roads to the old port, and the silence of ice fell on the ship. The generators thrummed but did not dent it. The clouds stacked themselves grey and solid. Seabirds came and screamed over the bridge; the crew played cards and lost their wages. The floes fused and the silence deepened. The cargo — coke and coal — settled in the holds. I iced myself in as the ship iced herself in and we watched each other. It was a sweet solution.

'Three minutes...'

I sat in my cabin and read *The Thirty-Nine Steps*. I remember hearing the words in my head but the silence filled me. It was a silence of cold and loss, Isabel's silence and the silence of my heart. Most of all it was the silence of regret, the one that comes when you know you have wronged someone close. I was that someone. I did not want to know myself. I would wash my hands for no reason at all and never touch another woman. My breath steamed and I heard the ship strain against the thickening ice. I wanted to strip and lie on it, I wanted to turn blue and die in two minutes flat. I wanted...

'Last page...'

How long had it been, how long since I had felt I could hold a woman and not disgust myself with the thought that I was using her, buying her, trading hearts on a one-way voyage? I felt my heart calm now, and as she finished the chapter I took my hand from my shirt and rested it in my lap. She closed the book, laid it on the floor and turned towards me.

'Tell me how good it is,' she said. 'How good can you make me feel, Michael?'

'It's the best film you've ever made. It was wonderful, you were wonderful. You were Jennifer.'

'Thanks…'

'You are wonderful. You're going to win an Oscar.'

'You reckon?'

'Absolutely. No contest…'

She laughed. 'Sure.'

'And Robert Mitchum. He was always my favourite actor. What a face! His eyelids are…'

'Forget Bob,' she said.

'Gone,' I said, and I clicked my fingers. 'Gone, forgotten. But not for ever…'

'No.'

Our faces were a foot apart. I moved an inch towards her and she moved too, but then I stopped. This was close and serious and I tried to count the years since the last time I had done this, since the iced-up years I gave myself. Thirty years. What sort of solution were they? Why did I freeze myself? I had no excuse, and then a man has forgotten the moves. He knows it's happening as it does, but he thinks that maybe it's a blessing. No more monkey on your back. No more waiting in darkened alleys for light footsteps that will never come, no more standing beneath balconies with your face turned to the moon. Guilty feelings, dead dreams in a damp bed…

'Elizabeth?' I said.

'Yeah?'

'I stayed to watch the credits, but Mrs Bell didn't. She waited for me outside. I don't think she liked me for that. She said she caught a chill.'

'Little things shouldn't come between lovers.'

'What do you mean? We're not lovers…'

'It's what I learned, Michael. You know me.' She winked. 'Turn me upside down and use me as a champagne glass.'

'What?'

'I smoke twenty-five to thirty a day, drink enough liquor to stone a horse, I've been married twice, three times, I can never remember. A couple of them kinda merged into each other. But I'm seventy-five years old.' She raised a finger and wagged it at me. 'And I don't care.' She put the finger away. 'You could have stayed for the credits or left halfway through the movie and gone for a pizza instead. I'd still go for you.'

'Go for me?'

'Sure.'

'Would you?'

'Please,' she said, 'you know that,' and she took my hand. 'You're boiling!' She put her other hand on my forehead. 'Are you sick? I know that look.'

'What look?'

'Your skin! You want to lie down…'

'I'm okay. Fine.'

'You don't look fine. You should go to bed…'

'Please!' I raised my voice. 'Maybe I felt a little twinge, but I have one of them every day. It's my body talking to me, giving me the warning I'm supposed to listen to.'

'And do you?'

'Of course. I'm not an idiot. I've been one. I know the feeling.' I tapped my heart. 'It's in here, Elizabeth. It's woken up.'

'Your heart's been asleep?'

'For years,' I said.

'What's done the trick?'

'You have to ask?'

'No,' she said, 'but I want to hear you say it.'

'Come on, then,' I said. 'Come with me,' and I stood up and pulled her to me. She waited while I prodded the fire and then she let me lead the way.

21

A man forgets the moves and when he's sixty-eight and the estuaries of his heart have laid silt in all the important places then it's hard to remember, hard to dredge those places and remember what a woman's skin needs. A woman's skin needs tracing, a man's heart needs holding, a woman's eyes must be kissed, a man's hands must be smoothed, a woman's flight is longer, a man's glide is uncontrolled. I lay in bed with Elizabeth Green, and all my dreams carefully laid themselves at my feet, and the ice floes that once held me so tight cracked and broke around the bed. I heard them and she watched me as I listened. She blinked her huge eyes slowly, and their colour did not fail her. The wind blew against the plastic over the window, and salt spray drifted off the bay.

I moved slowly from disbelief to shock. As she rested her head on my chest and twirled the hairs there I felt my life contracting, time shrinking, memories overlapping and snapping under their accumulated weight. I heard her say, 'This is the night I've waited for,' and I heard the words echo back with my mother's voice. I heard my mother say, 'Always wear it. Promise me, Michael,' and I heard the sounds of a wharf at night, sailors pushing past, the hoot of a distant horn.

'I've forgotten something,' I said.

'What?'

'My cap. It's downstairs.' I took her hand and kissed it and laid it on the blanket, slipped out of bed and went to the door.

'Your cap?'

I turned and nodded.

'You're kidding!'

I opened the door, said, 'You won't know I've gone,' and went downstairs.

The wind was gusting, blowing west from the point to Port Juliet, strengthening and creaking the front door. Gloria was lying in front of the fire. She opened one eye and moved her head towards me. The first sheet of rain swept against the house, and the draught under the door picked up. I took my cap from its hook, put it on my head and said 'Go to sleep' to the dog. She closed her eye and I went back upstairs. I climbed into bed again, slipped an arm around Elizabeth Green and she rested her head on my shoulder.

'So what's with the cap?'

I thought and I waited, and I shifted towards her as I said, 'My mother gave it to me.' I took it off, turned it over and ran my fingers over the lining. I could feel the caul in there, smooth where it capped my head, wrinkled around the edges. It was the size of a fried egg. 'A sailor's cap. She bought it for me when I was born. I've had it mended a few times.'

'Can I see?'

'It's a part of me,' I said, and I gave it to her.

She rubbed its edges, its peak and the seams around the top. She held it to her nose and took a deep breath.

'It's as old as me.'

'You smell better.'

'My caul's stitched into the lining.'

'Your what?'

'My caul. You know...'

'No...'

'The membrane in the womb. I was born in it, I was born in a shroud. I came as I'll go. Born breathing water, Elizabeth. It hardly ever happens, but when it does it's as lucky as you can get. A baby born in its caul will never be drowned, and a sailor who owns a caul will never be drowned. I've got double luck.'

'So it protected you?'

'Most of the time. At sea, all of the time...'

'And you wear it in bed?'

'Only when I'm with a woman. You know... women and the sea...'

'What about them?'

'They're supposed to be similar.'

'Are they? Who says?'

'No one says, exactly.'

She turned and rubbed her lips over my chin. 'Did it protect you at sea?'

'Yes. I believe it did...'

'In bed?'

'No.'

'So women and the sea, they're not similar at all.'

I shrugged and said I didn't know, and didn't want to know. I was alive and that counted for more than the cap or the caul. She agreed with that, and tucked her knees up towards my waist. We kissed each other and then we did what old people do for loving. The wind blew through our moves, and the rain beat like rattles against the plastic. The slates drummed, the sea smashed the shore. The bed groaned like a ship, and all the time I felt my cap on my head and her in my arms and for once I felt protected, quiet in the cradle of luck and chance and their conjunction over Port Juliet in the early stormy spring of the year.

She dozed and then she slept, and I tucked a pillow under my head and watched her. The rain eased and a slice of moonlight caught her face for five minutes, and her face blued in my bed. There was never a chance that we would do what we could have done once but I did think the thought, I did imagine her running her fingers down my back. Like her voice the thought was an echo, lost at sea, sliding down the valleys of waves and foaming at the bottom. Elizabeth Green in my bed — that would be something to tell Mr Boundy. Elizabeth Green, that woman, that whore with her hair and her diamond brooch, and her voice. Elizabeth Green thinking that she's better than the rest of us, that she can buy love and respect. The wind raced on and the rain stormed over the house. I bent my head and kissed her cheek and like the dog she opened one eye and moved her head to look at me.

The older you are the more lightly you sleep, and the more lightly you sleep the flightier the dreams. She said, 'I was dreaming about the old days.'

I said, 'I haven't slept...'

'I was in this house I used to own. Miserable place, it was. Miserable times. Nineteen eighty? I don't know... I was in the kitchen, staring out at the back yard when a delivery man came by, put a package on the back step and tapped on the window. I had to sign for the package, and as I did he said, "You... you used to be Elizabeth Green, didn't you?", as if I was dead already. And I knew it, in the dream... I knew I was dead. I could eat and drink and breathe but I was dead inside.' She tapped her chest. 'As I was watching him leave I felt so sad, overwhelmingly sad. Sad like some lost child. That was it...'

'You cried in the night.'

'What does it mean?'

'Does it have to mean anything?'

'Sure.'

'I don't think so. The only thing that means anything, that matters, is that you're leaving today.'

'Am I?'

'Please...' I said.

'What?'

'Never mind.'

She smiled, half at me and half at the pillow, and said, 'I can't say what'll happen. This is a waking dream, isn't it? Who knows how it's going to end?'

I cannot say what will happen — I was not going to hang on to those words again. I would not fool myself again. She ran her tongue over her teeth and closed her eye, and five minutes later she was snuffling back to sleep. The storm gathered at the doors and windows of my house, and it flipped bricks from the

155

ruins and tossed them on to the shore. I listened for as long as I could, but some time before two o'clock in the morning I fell into my own dreaming, and lost all the sense waking gave me.

22

I made captain in 1972. I bought myself a new suit, a travelling clock/barometer/thermometer and a leather suitcase. This suitcase, the certification and my age kicked me into a gear I had never tried before, a stern one with narrow eyes, slitty lips and a lonely walk. The captain's walk, hands held behind the back, head up, the one I had been born for. I grew my first beard since Barcelona, Isabel and the plane trees of Sant Feliu de Guixols, and I told myself that I had not failed. I was not lonely; I was respected. Men waited for me to speak, and listened when I did. I was an artist of command, fearless, equal to any situation. My heart slept but I was a complete man, and all my ambitions had hatched.

I took my first command to West Africa, and as we swung at anchor in the Takoradi roads I stood on the bridge with my head over the radar screen, and I plotted the courses of a dozen ships as they crossed the Gulf of Guinea. I was at the centre of the screen, the ocean, the world. I was not proud but I was absolute. I was wearing tropical uniform: white sleeveless shirt, white trousers. I was not sweating. My first ship; she was the MV *Moon Dreams*, and we carried a mixed cargo from Tilbury. Tyres, stationery, twelve diesel generators, five second-hand Land Rovers, oil tanks and containers of small tools.

There's a place on the ocean where Europe fades, the swells lengthen and Africa begins to thrum, dimly at first, then stronger and deeper. One month this place is moving over the Cape St Vincent Ridge and the next it has drifted south to Madeira and it's there you feel it, there you smell the spiced steam that blows off the coast, the coast that gives more sailors more nightmares than nightmares exist. Even now, even with maps and radio, I have heard them whispering in their cabins, and they dream: creeping disease, solid water, cats the size of dogs and dogs the size of horses. Clouds that take the shape of monsters and spirits, beasts that eat Christians and Christians who cannot see an end to it. Clouds that fool and clouds that lie. Clouds no man could follow, however much he thought he knew them.

I left the radar and went to the bridge wing. I stood with my back to the sun and watched Ghana slip into the evening. Haze rose over the reefs and birds called from the trees that lined the shore. The sky bled the ocean, and fish jumped across the bows of the ship. The air was still but it passed me by. The holds creaked and a fetid smell drifted, but I stood apart. This bridge was mine, this world was mine, I was in control, I would not bend again. I heard the motorman call out. He was looking for the man who should have greased a bearing. He was doing his job and I was doing mine, and I would. I was stronger than I had ever been, and quieter in my mind. Memories came but I let them pass me by. I could not let them distract me. Not now, not here at the top of my life. I went back to the radar and its light crossed my face, around and around, and the courses of the ships in the Gulf blinked off, on, off and on.

Sunday morning boomed over the ruins. The storm passed. The sky spread itself, the sun rose milky and a bright sea foamed to the shore. Broken altocumulus spread from the west, the kindest clouds, spreading long shadows across the fields, the walls and my house. Gulls wailed with a light wind and the grass rustled along the verges of the road to Port Juliet.

I woke before Elizabeth Green. She was wearing one of my shirts. It had fallen off her shoulder and the buttons had come undone. I reached over and covered her up, and touched her cheek with my fingertips. She stirred but did not wake.

She had been in the film I had seen the night before, fifteen feet tall with shining teeth, huge eyes and hair like a twenty-five-year-old's. She had lived in my house for four days. We had gone for walks and watched gulls over the offshore stacks. I had taken her swimming in the sea and she had worn my clothes. We had eaten eggs together and worked in the vegetable garden. The sun had shone and it had rained, but she never mentioned the weather. She did not babble or crunch or say something stupid at the wrong moment. The little wattles of skin beneath her chin hung from her like leaves. Her lips quivered as she slept, and I noticed a mole beneath her left earlobe. It had a single fair hair growing from its centre. I held my fingers over it for a second then climbed slowly out of bed, grabbed my jacket and trousers and went downstairs. I dressed, put the kettle on the stove, then stepped outside with Gloria, and walked down to the shore.

As we passed the weavers' cottages I saw the cat crouched over the remains of a bird. It had been a wren. I recognised the feathers. Any sailor does. They are lucky; not as lucky or permanent as the best luck, but you don't pass them by.

Jenny's feather... Once upon a time, a beautiful mermaid sat upon her rock and sang with a voice so wondrous that passing sailors could not resist. They steered their ships closer and closer to the rock, for they wanted to hear more, and they wanted to see more, but lust for song and flesh brings its own terrible rewards and they were drowned, one after another.

A knight errant, a brave man whose name is lost in the faint clouds of time, determined to punish the wicked mermaid, but just as he was about to put his plan (details lost also) into action, the mermaid changed into a wren.

Infuriated beyond belief, the knight called upon higher powers, who placated his anger by condemning the mermaid to appear as a wren every New Year's Day...

I hissed the cat away, picked up the remains and plucked out a pair of tail feathers, wiped them clean on my sleeve and tucked them behind my ear. One, two, three, Jenny Jenny wren; a great deal smaller than a gull or a hen.

I walked down to the beach, stood with my back to the ocean, and as Gloria dashed to the tideline I shaded my eyes and stared towards the house.

I remember very well:

I thought about you sleeping through that morning, and I wished your mother had never left this place. I wished that luck or something stronger had given us a chance. Luck is an expression of man's ignorance? I don't think so. I think luck is like the wind blowing clouds.

Were you awake? Had you got out of bed? Were you peeking through a gap in the plastic? Had you brushed your hair? Could you see me? Did you decide to stay but quickly dismiss the thought? Did you think I looked handsome as I stood on the shore with the dog beside me? Did you turn around, pick up the black dress you arrived in, fold it up and put it in a bag? Did you?

Nothing changes for ever. Oh, please. You always find yourself back where you started, back at the place where the pain is keenest, and all your sense breaks and you could be twenty-five again. Did you think you were twenty-five again? Or were we old people? Was I a big old man with a regret denied and a dog? Did my hair make you think of clouds?

I remember; I thought about you sleeping through that morning, and I wished your mother had never left this place. I loved you because I had to. I know I was a selfish man but I had failed too many times and I wanted to know how that love you talked about felt. Unconditional love. Love for the end of our lives. I walked back to the house with a strained heart, but when I saw you the only thing I could say was:

'Good morning.'

'Hello.' She stretched and yawned, and her hair lay on her shoulders. I passed her a cup of lemon tea, and sat next to her on the bed. She put her hand on my knee and said, 'You'll have to get some music up here.'

'I was thinking about it.'

'Get a CD player.'

'I was reading about CDs. They sound very good.'

'They are,' she said, and she sipped her tea.

I reached behind my ear and took the wren's feathers, and held one out to her.

'What's this?'

'It's for you,' I said. 'It's the second luckiest thing a sailor can wear. I found it outside your mother's cottage.' I twirled it. 'Jenny's feather. You wear it in your cap. Or your hair.'

'Jenny's feather?'

'It's from a wren. I should have found it on New Year's Day, but…'

'Don't…' She held up a hand. '… explain,' and she brushed it against her lips. 'It's a sailor's charm?'

'Yes.'

'That's all I need to know.'

That was all you needed to know? I think you needed to know more but I couldn't tell you, I couldn't explain. Do you remember what I did instead? I went downstairs.

23

Jacob Green, mad as a kick and twice as hard, arrived to collect his mother from Port Juliet at half past twelve in the afternoon. Angie Kihn, a blonde woman, was with him. She was first out of the car. He sat behind the wheel for a minute, looking for me. I was in the vegetable garden with Elizabeth. We were hoeing and raking, and I was showing her how to sow a straight line of cabbage seed. I had stretched a line, trampled the soil and drawn the edge of the hoe from one end to the other. When I heard the car I went to the corner of the garden, watched for a moment and said, 'They're here.' I went to a corner of the garden and stood where I could watch but not be seen.

'Screw them,' she said, not angrily, but quietly, as if she'd hoped they'd forgotten or the world was no longer turning and no one cared any more. Silent stars, a blank sea, the final cloud. A desperate look.

I watched Jacob get out of the car. He slammed the door and called to Angie. She had already stumbled in her shoes, and was standing on one leg, holding the shoe in one hand, trying to straighten the heel. Their voices carried to where we were, but nothing distinct, I couldn't understand a word. Angie cupped her hands over her mouth and yelled, 'Hello! Elizabeth!'

'I'd better go down.' Elizabeth was standing next to me, holding a rake. I was wearing my wren's feather in my cap; she was wearing hers in her hair. We could have been a painting by an artist whose name I can't remember. I smelt her and she smelt me, and when the wind blew it blew our hair together.

Angie shaded her eyes and yelled louder. 'Elizabeth! Where are you?'

'I know what's going to happen,' I said.

'What?'

'When you go down there you're not coming back.' I put my hand on her arm. 'I know...'

'What?' she said.

What? You know. I don't believe in stories, I don't believe in tales; you haven't got a hammer, I didn't bring the nails.

I said, 'I've got less than a minute left with you.'

'You think so?'

'What else can I think?'

'Would you believe me if I told you I was scared?'

'Of me?'

'Please...'

'Of them?'

'Michael?' She narrowed her eyes at the ocean and the sky, and sighed. 'It came back to me, all that stuff I felt in Baja, and then yesterday. Yesterday, in my mother's cottage. I thought — I've come back for her. That's my cottage.' She looked down at it. 'I missed the chance once.' She tapped her chest. 'It's something in here, something strong. I want to learn to grow vegetables. I still want a life like this. I'm scared of leaving.' She pointed towards Jacob. 'And I'm not the crazy he thinks I am.'

'But?' I smiled.

'Are you laughing at me?'

'No,' I said. 'Never. Only with you.'

Angie called again, 'Elizabeth!', and started walking towards the house. Jacob said something we couldn't hear, but she waved him away.

I said, 'Can I tell you a story?'

'Sure.' She gave me a nod.

'When I was a young man I studied navigation. European navigation. That means bearings and soundings. Mathematics. Longitude, latitude, angular distances and great circles. The course of the stars. The critical element was always precision. My instincts fought precision but lost. My heart was ruled by numbers.'

'So?'

'So in 1982 I met a man called Mak. Mak Dolu. He was from Papua. He'd been taught Polynesian navigation. He told me to forget my charts, drop my dividers, lose my compass, forget the numbers. He pointed at the sea and said, "Read it, not a piece of paper. The swells, the colour of the water, the smell of it. The flight of birds..." '

'The colour of the water?'

'Yes. I didn't believe it, but he had more.'

'What more?'

'The shape of clouds.'

'Clouds?'

'He had used nothing but the shape of clouds to navigate an open boat from Fangataufa to Yokahama, via Vanuata and the islands of the Coral Sea. That's thousands of miles. The shape of clouds telling you that you were twenty-eight nautical miles off the coast of Guadalcanal? We argued. I said it was impossible. He smiled. I told him that an open boat was different to eighteen thousand tons of cargo vessel, but he shook his head and said, "It is exactly the same sea. The same sky..." '

Elizabeth said, 'It's a nice story, but what's it got to do with us?'

Us.

'He was right. I was right too, my navigation was more precise, but his had a fix on something else, something more important than precision. Something elemental.'

'He was right? You were right? Cut to the chase, Michael.'

'At the time I thought about leaving the merchant navy. I'd been a captain for ten years. I'd achieved my ambition but I was missing something.' I spread my arms. 'Something like this. I dreamed of quitting and moving to Polynesia and buying a yacht. I was going to live another life. Live on the boat and run charters between the islands. Pleasure trips, anything. I was going to do what you almost did in Baja. I regretted not taking the chance, not as much as I regret some things, but you think, don't you? You wonder how your life could have been.'

'You bet.'

'The sea stole me. I had a lot of catching up to do. I wanted to learn to read the shape of the clouds.'

She pointed at the sky. 'That one looks like a horse's head. See?'

'But what does it mean?'

'I don't know...'

163

I interrupted, took her hand and said, 'We've wanted the same thing all our lives.'

'Michael...' she said, and her eyes dulled and she had to turn away. 'Staying's not as easy as thinking. Or dreaming.'

She had said that before and I had told her not to think about it but now all I could manage was, 'Go to them. No goodbyes.'

'I can't just...'

'Don't keep them waiting.'

'What do I say? What do I tell them?' She looked up at me and I wanted her eyes.

I whispered, 'I love you.'

She shook her head. 'You don't know me.'

'I do.'

'How can you?'

'I'm an old man, Elizabeth. Old enough to know whatever I want. And that cloud...' I pointed. 'That's not a horse's head...'

'Tell me.'

'What?'

'He thinks I'm mad.' She looked down at Jacob. 'Is he right?'

'He doesn't know anything.'

'Am I old enough to know better than this?'

'Than what?'

'I'm having doubts,' she said.

'About what?'

She said, 'Tell me you love me.'

'I do love you.'

She reached out and stroked my face. 'You mean it. You mean what you say, don't you?'

I nodded.

'I don't think anyone's meant it before.'

'Should I be pleased? Is there hope for me?'

'Of course there is,' she said, and, 'You're right. I have to go to them.' She passed me the rake. It was warm where she had held it. Our fingers touched, and then she turned from me and walked away from the vegetable garden, down the path to the house.

I walked to a place on the cliffs, a pulpit of grass with a view of the ruins, the beach, the offshore stacks and the distant point. I sat down and watched Elizabeth strolling away from the garden, down to the house and into her agent's arms. They kissed and I heard a yelp of excitement, then nothing. Jacob stood to one side, and when the two women began to walk, he kept up with them, but at a distance.

I felt like the captain of a ship with a shifting cargo, high above a crew I could not control. A crew with ideas of their own, talking a language I did not understand. They crossed the yard, disappeared behind the cottages and emerged on the beach, and began to walk away from me. The sea sucked, the wind blew, I forgot that I was holding the rake. Lonely as hell, lost as a small animal that lived in the garden wall. Sunk. I took my cap off and held it to my chest, and I recalled the times when it had protected me. I whispered to it as I watched them walk to the end of the beach, stop and turn. I held it to my ear, I listened to it, I fingered the stitching and then I began to pick at it. First one strand of cotton broke, then another, then another, then another, then another, another and I had half the inside lining in my hand. Inside the lining was a circular envelope of padding, also stitched. I pulled this out and picked at the cotton that bound it. Then I was tearing the cotton and the padding was shredding and then I had my own caul in my hand and the cap was in bits on the ground.

It was brown, translucent in the middle, darkening to the edges, crinkled at the edges, smooth in the middle. It could have been one of those hide chews you can buy for your dog. I held it to my nose. It smelt of bedtime as a child, salt and hair. Chocolate and dust, envelopes and the backs of bottom drawers. When I tapped it with my fingernail it sounded as hollow as I felt, and echoed with voices from years back. There was the midwife clicking her tongue against the roof of her mouth, and there was my mother telling the daft woman to wrap me in something dry and not be so slow. Here, in a boom, was the bomb that ripped a hole in the side of the SS *Filles de Kilimanjaro*, and here was Miss Joyce of Shadwell saying, 'I think you should take him to the country.' Here she was, thinking she knew best, everyone thinking they knew best.

The last brush of my mother's lips, the letters she wrote, the cap she gave me pressed against my skin in the Baltic storm. The news of her death. Was I protected from that? Was I protected from anything? Was my great luck something I imagined, nothing but something to weigh against misfortune?

For a moment, a dead second, I almost threw the caul to the wind. I was turning it over in my hands, holding it to the light, listening to it again, watching the figures on the beach disappear, hearing the voices in my head fade. But I stopped myself, I put the thing in my pocket, picked up the remains of the cap and went back to the garden.

24

I took my last voyage in the spring of 1991, the MV *Spanish Key* out of Felixstowe to Gydnia via Copenhagen. A mixed cargo, a Polish crew, the clouds impossible to read. Nothing but lowering stratocumulus.

I remember — the crew were sympathetic. They kept out of my way, they gave me the run of the bridge. I ate alone in the day cabin, and didn't raise my voice.

Through the gas fields of the North Sea and the cloud broke. Past the nervous coast of Denmark, Helsingør Castle floodlit in the night, crates of beer stacked on the quay at Copenhagen, the sound of the crew cheering a woman as she waved from the deck of a sail training ship...

The Baltic... it was calm and blue, and with the *Spanish Key* on automatic pilot I sat back in the helmsman's chair. The ocean spread before me, the sun above, seabirds drifting. The crackle of the radio, the sweep of the radar, the blink of a dozen lights. The horizon dulled into the sky while Poland grew to the south.

I was experienced, trusted with twelve thousand tons of cargo ship and a crew of eighteen men. I had money in the bank and luck drifted in my wake. Some women had remembered me; dogs liked me. I had no unsavoury personal habits, and I did not hold grudges. I did not believe in God but I read at least one book a week. I had never been unemployed but I had never worked on land. The sea owned me, and as it washed by I wished it would tell me what I was going to do. Where could I go? Would I die without it; would my luck dry up? Had I made a mistake; should I have bought a yacht and sailed the islands of Polynesia? Should I buy a dog?

I got down from the helmsman's chair and stood over the chart table. I picked up the dividers and checked the position. Perfect. I looked outside and checked the clouds. Exactly fourteen nautical miles off Rozewie, entering the Gulf of Danzig.

I spent my last run ashore in Gdansk. I drank coffee and ate a pastry in a main street café, an expensive place with huge tables and carved chairs. The smell of a sweet perfume hung in the air.

I went to the cinema and saw a Polish film about an apple picker, a piano player and the rites of spring. I didn't understand a word but I enjoyed it, I enjoyed the dark. I felt slow and as I watched the credits I wanted to stay where I was, I did not want to go home.

'I retired on the first day of May.

'I took a train from Felixstowe to London, and visited my mother's grave. It was raining. Her stone and the earth told

me nothing. I laid some flowers on the grass, but as I was doing it I felt bad and empty. I wanted to talk to her, to tell her
that her cap had protected me, and I wanted to ask her what
I should do. I wanted to get down on my knees but I couldn't
bend, the words broke, the thoughts faded away. I walked away
with no idea.

'I had a niece in Liverpool. I phoned her and she invited me to
stay, but when we met I didn't recognise her and we had nothing
to say. She watched television during the day and stayed out
all night, every night. She didn't have a book in the house, or
any pictures on the walls. So I packed my sea-bag, left a note
on her kitchen table and began to voyage through the country.

'As I travelled, I followed the direction of clouds. When I left
Liverpool they were drifting north-east, so I walked towards
the Yorkshire Dales, and I got work building a wall. Later the
clouds blew to the west, and I blew to the Lakes. I loved the
Lakes. You'd love the Lakes...

'I worked for a boatman at Coniston. It was my job to take
money from tourists who wanted to rent rowing boats on the
lake. I enjoyed that. I stayed for the summer. I let the clouds
drift without me.'

'Then...'

'One foot in front of the other.

'The autumn came and I followed a flight of cirrus south.
I think I ended up in Wales. I remember painting a farmer's
caravan and playing with his dogs on the beach. Or maybe he
only had one dog... I remember the place, though, in Dyfed.
It was along the coast from Fishguard.

'I became a story sailors tell, the one about the old captain
who travels the earth looking for the comfort the ocean used
to give him, reading the shape of clouds as he once read the
swell of waves. He stands at crossroads and can hear waves as
they break a hundred miles away, and he always heads towards
them. He carries a shell in his pocket and wears a cauled cap on

his head.' I put my hand in my pocket and pulled out a shell. I put it on the bed. 'That's it.

'One day a cloud drifted here and stopped, and it chose this place for me. West as feet can follow, the sea a pool of tears... It told me to rest and I thought, *I've done enough walking. That's enough*. The cloud moved on but I stayed. I bought the house, I started the garden, I frightened the natives and then...'

'What?'

'You came.' I took her hand and she rested her head on my shoulder. 'You came.'

She said, 'I almost didn't.'

I had put glass in the windows. A single cloud crossed the face of the moon. Its shadow caught the side of the house and spilled into the bedroom. We watched it cross the floor and spread up the far wall before fading.

'But you did.'

'I did,' she said, as another cloud shadowed the room.

I lay back and listened to the sea rustling along the shore, and the call of a distant bird. I shifted my legs and she shifted towards me, and when I closed my eyes I heard the darkness sing, and the clouds gathered in chorus.

This was in the night of the late spring. The air was cool but had begun to sense summer. The bird's call was returned by a cry from the ruins, a single note that held itself for a moment and then faded away.

Peter Benson's new novel
OUT IN AUGUST 2012

David Morris lives the quiet life of a book-valuer for a London auction house, travelling every day by omnibus to his office in the Strand. When he is asked to make a trip to rural Somerset to value the library of the recently deceased Lord Buff-Orpington, the sense of trepidation he feels as he heads into the country is confirmed the moment he reaches his destination, the dark and impoverished village of Ashbrittle. These feelings turn to dread when he meets the enigmatic Professor Richard Hunt and catches a glimpse of a screaming woman he keeps prisoner in his house.

Peter Benson's new novel is a slick gothic tale in the English tradition, a murder mystery, a reflection on the works of the masters of the French Enlightenment and a tour of Edwardian England. More than this, it is a work of atmosphere and unease which creates a world of inhuman anxiety and suspense.

978-1-84688-206-7 • 250 pp. • £14.99

Also available by Peter Benson

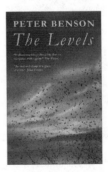

Winner of the Encore Award, a trenchant critique of modern civilization, describing how one family's tropical heaven becomes hell.

978-1-84688-192-3
144 pp. • £8.99

Winner of the *Guardian* Fiction Prize, a lyrical portrait of the landscape of the Somerset Levels and a touching evocation of first love.

978-1-84688-191-6
160 pp. • £8.99

Winner of the Somerset Maugham Award, a novel exploring the evolution of an unlikely relationship, in a beautiful countryside setting.

978-1-84688-193-0
144 pp. • £8.99

The gripping tale of a quiet and solitary private detective whose uneventful life world spirals into a circle of chaos and death.

978-1-84688-196-1
192 pp. • £8.99

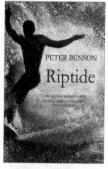

A compelling tale of surfing and coming of age, and an intense examination of a young man's struggle to establish his identity.

978-1-84688-195-4
192 pp. • £8.99

Weaving in the dramatic events portrayed by the Bayeux Tapestry, an absorbing novel which brings to life a fascinating period of English history.

978-1-84688-194-7
240 pp. • £8.99